"At least you survived your first date with me."

Luke grinned at her, hoping to lighten the mood.

She laughed. She had a nice laugh. It was light and musical and easy on the ears. "I survived thanks to you protecting me." Her gaze was warm on him. "Thank you, Luke, for throwing me down and using yourself as a shield to protect me. That's real hero material as far as I'm concerned."

"Hell, Carrie. I'm no hero. I'm just a man on a mission to find my father's killer."

REVENGE ON THE RANCH

New York Times Bestselling Author
CARLA CASSIDY

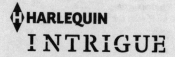

HARLEQUIN
INTRIGUE

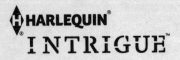

ISBN-13: 978-1-335-58209-6

Revenge on the Ranch

Copyright © 2022 by Carla Bracale

Recycling programs
for this product may
not exist in your area.

For questions and comments about the quality of this book, please contact us at CustomerService@Harlequin.com.

Harlequin Enterprises ULC
22 Adelaide St. West, 41st Floor
Toronto, Ontario M5H 4E3, Canada
www.Harlequin.com

Printed in U.S.A.

Carla Cassidy is an award-winning, *New York Times* bestselling author who has written over 170 books, including 150 for Harlequin. She has won the Centennial Award from Romance Writers of America. Most recently she won the 2019 Write Touch Readers Award for her Harlequin Intrigue title *Desperate Strangers*. Carla believes the only thing better than curling up with a good book is sitting down at the computer with a good story to write.

Books by Carla Cassidy

Harlequin Intrigue

Kings of Coyote Creek

Scene of the Crime

Visit the Author Profile page at Harlequin.com.

CAST OF CHARACTERS

Luke King—He's a man on a mission...determined to find his father's murderer.

Carrie Carlson—She's determined to help Luke fulfill his goal. Maybe then he'll realize her true feelings for him.

Peter Jeffries—Luke believes he is the guilty party.

Dr. Raymond Stillson—Has the doctor's obsession with Carrie turned deadly?

Caleb King—Luke's younger brother. Did he kill his father?

Leroy Hicks—Did the former ranch hand kill the man who fired him?

Chapter One

Luke King raced silently across the tall prairie grass, grateful that there was very little moonlight tonight. It was just after 2:00 a.m. on a Saturday, and as he headed toward Wayne Bridges's barn, his heart beat rapidly. Every nerve and muscle in his body was taut with tension. Even the cool early-June night air couldn't chill the fire that burned in his gut.

Tonight, he was hoping to find the evidence he needed to put his father's murderer behind bars. A little over two months ago, Big John King had been shot dead in his driveway, sending Luke's entire family into a tailspin of confusion and grief.

Even now, just thinking about his father shot a shaft of deep anguish through him. His grief had turned into a ball of rage that never left his chest, a rage that threatened to consume him all the time.

He believed he knew the identity of the man who had shot his father. John King had been running for mayor of their small town of Coyote Creek, Kansas, at the time of his death. He had been running against two other men—fellow ranchers Wayne Bridges and Joe Daniels.

Everyone believed that Big John would be the next mayor, and Luke believed Wayne wanted his father dead and permanently out of the race. He had a very strong hunch that Wayne had hired one of his ranch hands to pull the trigger.

Luke jumped behind a tree as he got closer to Wayne's barn door. He could now hear the men inside, their boisterous, drunken voices and laughter drifting outside the partially open door. He'd followed them here from the Red Barn, a popular bar in town where they'd begun their drunken escapades.

He believed the actual shooter was Peter Jeffries, a particularly nasty man who was known as a champion sharpshooter and a big drunk.

Luke was betting that one night Peter, in one of his drunken hazes, would confess. He would probably boast to his fellow ranch hands about what he had done. And that's why Luke was here, eavesdropping on the drunken fools inside Wayne's barn. He'd been listening to them every Friday and Saturday night for the past two weeks, hoping to hear a drunken confession that he could take to Lane Caldwell, the chief of police.

He crept closer to the barn door and tried to pick

out Peter's voice among all the others. It sounded like there were four or five men inside laughing and talking. The current topic of conversation was the women in town.

"Give me some of that Heather Jacks," one of the men said. "Have you seen the rack on that woman?"

"Oh yeah, I'd like to order her right off the menu at the café," another voice said and laughed raucously.

Heather Jacks was a pretty waitress who worked at the café. Luke had gone out with her a couple of times. She was a nice young woman, but there had been no real sparks between them. Still, it fed his anger to hear the men talk about her like she was nothing more than a piece of meat.

He'd just moved a couple of steps closer when suddenly a big hand clamped down hard on his shoulder. "What have we here?" a deep voice growled.

Luke whirled around to come face-to-face with Sly Baskum, a big, burly man who worked for Wayne. "Hey, guys," he bellowed loudly. "Looks like we've got a spy out here."

Luke backed up as several of the other men exited the barn, their faces silhouetted by the bright barn light behind them. "Well, if it isn't one of those stinking Kings," one of them said.

Luke instantly smelled danger in the air. The

men were all liquored up and spoiling for a fight. "Did you lose your way, little boy?" another one of them said and poked Luke in the chest.

"Hey, man, don't touch me," Luke said as his heart beat frantically. Fight-or-flight adrenaline soared through him as the men circled around him.

"Don't touch you? Is that what you said, you little trespasser?" Sly pushed him from the back, causing him to fall into Peter Jeffries, Alan Kauffman and Jeff Tanner.

"Okay, I won't touch you… I'll punch you instead." Alan threw a fist that caught Luke in his stomach. The air whooshed out of Luke, and he heard the other men laugh uproariously.

Luke might have had a chance if the fight had been fair and one-on-one, but it was five against one, and as they began to pummel Luke, all he could do was fight back while at the same time trying to get away.

The punches came faster and faster, hitting him in his stomach and on his face and head. Pain roared through him, making him nauseous. The men all laughed, but their laughter was mean-spirited as they fed off each other's drunken energy.

An uppercut to his chin snapped his head back, and that was followed by a blow to Luke's stomach that sent him to his knees. The men then began to kick him. Why didn't they stop? They'd proved their point. He had been where he shouldn't have been.

He attempted to crawl away, but they followed him, still kicking and punching him. Boots connected over and over again with his ribs. Luke's only desire was to get away from the agonizing pain they were inflicting on him.

Nobody knew he was here…not his older brother, Johnny, or his younger brother, Caleb. Nobody was going to suddenly show up to save him, and if these men didn't stop, they were going to kill him.

He took a hard kick to the side of his head. Pain seared through him as stars danced dizzily in his brain. And then…nothing.

He awakened slowly, his body screaming with pain. Luke opened his eyes and stared in bewilderment at his surroundings. How had he gotten to the hospital? Why was he in the hospital and why was he hurting so badly?

For a moment his thoughts were completely confused. Had he been in a car accident? Or had he fallen off his horse? What in the hell had happened to him?

He closed his eyes and searched his brain, and then he remembered. He'd been at the Bridges barn, and the ranch hands there had given him one hell of a beating. So, how had he gotten to the hospital? He didn't believe any one of those men had brought him here.

His ribs were killing him, and he had a headache that torched pain through him each time he moved. Those men had really done a number on him.

He was now clad in a god-awful pale blue flowered hospital gowns with an IV running from the back of his hand to a bag on a stand next to his bed. So, how in the hell had he gotten here? The question kept repeating itself in his head.

A sound in his room snapped his eyes back open. It was Carrie Carlson, one of the nurses. "Luke, oh good. You're awake," she said. "How are you feeling?"

"Like a truck ran over me, a very big truck, and it ran over me more than once. How did I get here?" He pushed the button that raised the head of his bed.

"I wasn't here when you were brought in, but it's written in the notes that Jeb Taylor found you on the side of the road just outside your ranch. You were unconscious and had obviously been beaten badly, so he brought you straight here."

Jeb Taylor was the town handyman, but at that time on a Saturday night, he'd probably been going home from a friend's place. Luke would need to find the tall, bald man and thank him.

"Now, I need to take your vitals," Carrie said

and moved closer to the side of his bed. She scanned his forehead with the thermometer, and even that slight touch caused his head to pound unmercifully.

She then wrapped a blood pressure cuff around his arm. As she pumped it up, he gazed at her. He'd seen Carrie around town, but he didn't know her personally, and he definitely hadn't really noticed before just how pretty she was.

Her long, dark hair was pulled back into a low ponytail, and her blue-violet eyes had long, thick, dark eyelashes. When she leaned closer to him, he smelled the scent of her, a fragrance of flowers mingling with mysterious spices. It was a very attractive fragrance.

In another life, in another time, he might have flirted with her. He might have even asked her out on a date. But, in this life and in this time, romance and love were the very last things he had on his mind.

The only thing that ticked him off about last night was he now knew he wouldn't be able to eavesdrop at that barn and on those men anymore. He'd been busted, and there was no way he'd be able to sneak back there to listen to them again.

"I'm happy to give you some good news. I have a little pain relief to give you," she said with a smile. She had a very nice smile.

"I'll take it," Luke replied.

"I'm just going to administer it into your IV. You should feel some relief fairly quickly." She put the medicine in and then stepped back from the bed. "Is there anything I can do for you, Luke?"

Her gaze was soft, sympathetic, and once again he noticed how pretty she looked in the purple scrubs that turned her eyes more violet than blue.

"No, I'm good," he half growled, hating to be in such a state of weakness in front of anyone else.

"Dr. Reeves will be in to speak to you later."

He half nodded and then closed his eyes. True to what Carrie had said, within minutes he felt a softening of the jagged pain he'd awakened with.

He must have fallen asleep, for he jerked awake once again when he heard somebody entering his room. It was an older woman he didn't know, and she pushed a cart before her.

"How about some breakfast, handsome?" She smiled widely and grabbed a tray from the cart. "You've got scrambled eggs with crispy bacon, some toast and coffee. There's also grape jelly, and cream and sugar if you want it." She set the tray on the table that would slide across the bed.

"Thank you, ma'am," he said, surprised to realize that despite everything hurting, he had an appetite.

"You need anything else, handsome, you just press that little button and ask for Wanda. Wanda, that's me. Everyone here knows Wanda." She grinned at him again. "Now, get to eating while it's all hot."

The moment Wanda left his room, he took the lid off the coffee cup and took a sip, grateful that it was strong and good. He'd just finished cleaning his plate when Chief of Police Lane Caldwell walked into the room along with Luke's older brother, Johnny.

"I hope the other guy looks worse than you, but I'm not sure that's possible," Johnny said and sat in the chair next to the hospital bed. "So, what happened to you?"

Luke frowned. "I guess I got the hell beat out of me."

"Who did this to you, Luke?" Lane asked. He stood at the foot of the bed, a deeply concerned look on his face. Luke knew Lane was in his fifties, but in the last month or so, he seemed to have aged ten years. Apparently, the unsolved murder of Big John King, along with other cases he had, weighed heavily on him.

"How did you two even know I was here?" Luke asked curiously.

"Dr. Holloway called me when you were brought in late last night. He wouldn't allow me to speak to you then. I'm the one who called Johnny this morning to let him know you were here," Lane explained. "Now, want to tell me who did this to you, Luke?"

Luke winced as he changed positions in the bed. "It doesn't really matter who did it."

Johnny leaned forward in his chair. "Luke, it does matter. Whoever did this to you should face some criminal charges."

Luke laughed, instantly regretting it as his ribs protested with a searing pain. "Since when do we press charges for a fistfight around here? Besides, what happened was my own fault, and I take full responsibility for it. Lane, all I need from you is to find my father's murderer."

Luke hadn't really told Lane too much concerning his suspicions about Peter Jeffries. He didn't want Peter to be warned that he was under suspicion. Otherwise, Luke might not be able to get the evidence he needed.

"Are you sure you don't want to tell me who did this to you?" Lane asked with concern.

"I'm positive," Luke replied firmly.

"Okay, then I guess I'll just get out of here," Lane said.

"Now, tell me what really happened," Johnny said the moment Lane had left the room.

"There's nothing to tell. Just for your information, it was more than one man beating on me, and it happened because I was in the wrong place at the wrong time. And that's all I intend to say about the matter."

Johnny narrowed his eyes as he gazed at Luke.

"Luke, you've got to stop. I've told you before, leave the investigation to Lane."

"Yeah, because he's doing such a good job," Luke replied bitterly. "It's been a little over two months since somebody shot our father, and still nobody is under arrest. Hell, Lane doesn't even have any suspects."

"Luke, you've got to leave it alone. I don't know where you were last night or what you were doing, but you could have been killed. Do you hear me? You could have been killed."

"Okay, well, I wasn't," Luke replied.

"This time you weren't. Dammit, Luke, I need you on the ranch. You're supposed to be coming up with a plan for us to move forward with a horse-breeding program."

"I'll get to it. I've been working the ranch every day. What I do in my spare time is nobody's business," Luke snapped.

"Dammit, Luke, do you hear the rage in your voice?" Johnny asked. "You're being eaten alive by it."

"I'm done talking." Luke lowered the head of his bed and closed his eyes. He didn't want his brother to tell him what to do or how to think. Of course, Luke had a lot of rage inside him. Somebody had killed his father, and even getting the hell beaten out of him wouldn't stop Luke on his mission to get the person responsible behind bars.

CARRIE CARLSON LEFT the house she rented with fellow nurse and her good friend Emily Timmons. She got into her car, pulled out of the driveway and then headed down the tree-lined street toward the main drag.

It was a beautiful early-summer afternoon. The trees were filled with big fat leaves, and the grass had all turned a lush green after the long winter. It all felt like new beginnings, and in keeping with that, Carrie was about to do the most brazen, most forward thing she'd ever done in her life. She was going to check on a former patient at his home. More specifically, she was going to check on the man she'd had a crush on forever, Luke King.

He'd been released from the hospital two days before, after being diagnosed with a concussion, three fractured ribs and bruised kidneys. He'd also had various other contusions, including a rather nasty bruise on his lower jaw.

Before his father's death, Luke had had a reputation as a ladies' man. With his rich dark hair, beautiful blue eyes and handsomely sculpted features, he'd never had to beg for a date.

He also had wonderfully broad shoulders, slim hips and long legs. Physically he was the whole package. But as far as she knew, he hadn't dated anyone since his father's murder. And in a small town like Coyote Creek, where gossip ran rampant, she would have known.

She'd always hoped he would ask her out. He was friendly when they ran into each other in town, but he never seemed to see her as a woman to potentially date. Still, since his father's death, Carrie hadn't been able to get him out of her head, especially since he'd left the hospital pretty banged up.

She turned onto the two-lane road that would take her out to the King place. She rolled down her window and breathed in the outside air. It smelled like rich earth and sweet grass and cattle.

This was ranching country, and Big John King had left behind an empire. The Kings were one of the most successful operations in the state. With Big John dead, the bulk of the responsibility for the ranching would now fall on Johnny and Luke.

She wasn't sure what role the younger brother, Caleb, or their sister, Ashley, would have in the day-to-day running of the ranch. From the gossip she'd heard around town, Caleb was a self-proclaimed artist who drank too much. She knew Ashley owned a store in town, Bling and Things, that sold items for the home and a few nice clothes.

As she turned onto the long driveway that would eventually lead to Luke's home, her stomach clenched with nervous energy. She told herself all she wanted to do was check in with him and see how he was doing physically.

But the truth of the matter was she just wanted

to see him, and she was hoping he might suddenly see her as a potential woman to date. She knew it was probably a stupid idea, but she was doing it anyway.

She drove past the big King family house. It was a huge, rambling ranch. She had never been inside it before, but she'd heard it was absolutely beautiful. She couldn't help but think about poor Margaret King, who had not only recently gone through a bout with breast cancer but had then lost her husband in an instant to violence. The rumor in town was that she was absolutely broken.

All the King children lived on the ranch except Ashley, who had an apartment above her store. She'd had a house in town, but about a month ago she had sold it and made the move to her store.

The next house she passed was Johnny's. Although it was smaller than the big house, it was an attractive place. Her fingers tightened on the steering wheel as once again an attack of nerves fluttered through her.

Finally, she came to Luke's house. Tucked in among tall trees and with a pond nearby, the place looked like an enchanted cabin in the woods. Two wooden chairs with bright red pillows sat on one side of the covered porch, with a small table in between them.

She pulled up in front of it and parked. She'd worn jeans and a sleeveless pink blouse, knowing that it was a good color on her. She'd left her long hair loose and flowing around her shoulders. She'd also applied a little more makeup than she usually wore on a workday.

She turned off her engine and sat for just a few moments. She drew deep breaths in an effort to calm her nerves and then got out. It was two o'clock on a Tuesday afternoon. For all she knew, Luke was someplace on the ranch working—something the doctor had specifically told him not to do for at least a week to ten days.

Drawing another deep breath, she walked up to the front door and knocked. After a moment the door opened and Luke looked at her in surprise. "Carrie, what are you doing here?"

"I just thought I'd come by and see how you were getting along," she replied. Clad in a pair of worn jeans and with a white T-shirt stretching taut across his broad shoulders, he looked positively hunky. Even the purple bruise darkening his lower jaw couldn't detract from his handsomeness.

"Come on in," he said and opened the door wider to allow her entry.

As she swept past him, she caught the scent of minty soap mingling with a woodsy cologne emanating from him. It was definitely a pleasant scent. Once they were both inside, he gestured her toward a brown leather sofa, and he sat in a brown recliner facing her. Decorated in rich earth tones, the living room felt warm and inviting. There was a fire-place on one wall, and she could easily envision it filled with burning logs to warm a wintry night.

"Your home is really nice," she said.

"Thanks. I like it here."

"So, how are you feeling?" she asked.

"I'm feeling just fine."

She eyed him dubiously. "Luke, I know all the injuries you suffered. There's no way you're feeling just fine after two days."

He offered her a rueful grin. "Okay, I'm still hurting a bit, but I'll live."

Oh Lordy, when he smiled like that, he caused a warmth to pool in her lower belly. "Have you had any nausea or vomiting since you've been home?" she asked, momentarily putting on her nurse's hat.

"No, nothing like that. My only complaint is that I'm still pretty sore, especially in my ribs."

"Then you need to listen to your body and take it easy," she replied. "You went through a trauma, being beaten up like that, and the doctor told you not to do anything strenuous for at least a week."

"Trust me, I know, and I haven't done anything since I've been home. Uh…can I get you something to drink? Maybe a soda or some tea?" he asked.

"No, thanks, I'm fine."

For the next few minutes, they visited about the weather and things that were happening in town.

The conversation flowed surprisingly easily, even though on some level she couldn't quite believe she was actually sitting in Luke King's living room and talking to him.

"I should get out of here and let you rest. I really just wanted to stop by and see if you were doing okay," she said after about half an hour of visiting. She certainly didn't want to overstay her welcome.

His features pulled into a frown. "I won't be okay until the man who murdered my father is behind bars."

"Luke, I'm so sorry for your loss," she replied with all the compassion she had for him and his family. "I can't imagine the pain you've all been in."

"Thanks. I think he was murdered over a stupid mayoral seat. I think he was murdered because Wayne Bridges wanted him out of the way before the election. If he hadn't been killed, Dad would have definitely become the next mayor, and that was something Wayne wanted desperately." He frowned. "Sorry, I shouldn't be talking about all this with you."

"Luke, you can talk to me about anything at all. I consider this conversation and any other ones we might have between us to be confidential, and I would never betray your confidence."

His blue eyes gazed into hers intently for several long minutes. "Do you know Peter Jeffries?"

"I know him as a nasty man who is usually drunk and obnoxious at the Red Barn," she replied. "Why?"

He held her gaze once again for several long moments before replying. "I believe he's the man who shot my father. I think Wayne hired him to do the job." He swiped a hand down his face. "God, I've never said that aloud to anyone."

Carrie slowly digested what he had just told her. "So, did you fight with him? Is that what happened to you?"

"Him and four other men. I knew the men sometimes partied in Wayne's barn after spending the evening at the Red Barn. So, for the last two weekends, I've been eavesdropping outside Wayne's barn door to see if Peter would get drunk enough to admit to the other men that he pulled the trigger. That night they caught me outside their barn."

"Oh, Luke, they could have killed you," Carrie replied fervently.

He sat up straighter in the chair. "I don't care," he said roughly. "I need to get the proof that will put my father's killer in prison. It's been a little over two months, and Lane hasn't done anything. He has absolutely no clues at all. This is something I need to do. I know sooner or later Peter will get drunk enough to boast about what he did. I just need to be there when he does."

He slumped back, as if exhausted by his short

diatribe. Carrie's mind continued to whirl with everything he'd said. "You know, Peter drinks at the Red Barn almost every night of the week."

"Yeah, but I can't exactly sit next to him every time he's there. I would be really conspicuous."

"Maybe you wouldn't be as conspicuous if you were on a date," she replied. She was probably being stupid in offering what she was about to offer. He'd probably laugh in her face, but that didn't stop her from voicing what she was thinking.

"Luke, I'm starting a two-week vacation tomorrow. I would be available to go with you to the Red Barn anytime Peter is there. We could pretend we're dating, and we could try to sit as close to Peter as possible."

He didn't laugh at her. Instead, he straightened up once again and eyed her with interest. "That just might work," he said slowly. "Nobody would look sideways at us if we were on a date. Are you sure you really want to do this for me?"

"If it helps put a murderer behind bars, then absolutely, I'm in," she replied.

"I should probably tell you something else. It might be possible another person is responsible for my father's death." His forehead creased in another deep frown. "It's slightly possible my brother Caleb shot my father."

Carrie couldn't help the gasp of shock that escaped her. "What makes you think that?" she finally asked.

"He and Dad had a big fight the night before, and I don't know how much you listen to gossip, but Caleb isn't always in a rational frame of mind." The words seemed to come out of him slowly… painfully.

Once again, he stared at her in open speculation. "Maybe while we're pretending to date, you could hang out around here and see if you can get close to Caleb, maybe get him to confide in you."

"I guess I could try to do that," she replied. "I'll do whatever I can to help you, Luke."

"Why? Why would you agree to any of this?"

The question caught her by surprise. She couldn't very well tell him she was agreeing because she had a wild crush on him and this would be a way to spend time with him.

"I'm a nurse, Luke. I like to help people out, and it sounds like you need help," she finally replied.

"I don't know why I told you all this."

"Maybe it was a burden you needed to share and I just happened to come along at the right time."

"You're very easy to talk to, Carrie." He smiled at her once again, and again that flutter of sweet heat swept through her.

"Thanks, Luke," she replied. "And now I'd better get out of here and let you rest." She stood from the sofa, and at the same time he rose from his chair to walk her to the door.

"So, how about you come by here tomorrow right after dinner, say, around six? You can hang out here for a while and then we can head to the Red Barn," he said. His eyes held a brightness they hadn't had when she'd first arrived.

"I can do that," she agreed.

When they reached his front door, he held out a hand to her. She reached out her hand, and he clasped it tightly. "Then we're partners, right?" he asked.

"Definitely," she replied.

"And we can't tell anyone about the true intent of us being together," he added.

"That will be our secret. I told you that you can trust me, Luke."

Once again, his gaze held hers for several long moments. "I… I've needed somebody I can talk to…somebody to be on my side."

"I'm on your side, Luke, and hopefully we can get the creep who killed your father behind bars," she replied.

It was only a few minutes later, when she was on the drive back to her own place, that she thought about what she'd just agreed to. She must have been out of her mind to agree to this scheme. It could be a dangerous mission they'd set forward for themselves.

But she wasn't sorry. She had just set in motion a plan to spend lots of time with Luke. She was just hoping that in the process, he would not only see her as a partner in crime solving, but maybe also as a desirable woman he needed in his life.

Chapter Two

It was one of the longest days of Luke's life. He wasn't used to just sitting around his house and doing nothing, but he was taking the doctor's orders seriously, because his body told him he needed to take it easy. Another couple of days and he should be ready to get back to work on the ranch...at least, that's what he hoped.

Today the hours couldn't move fast enough until the time Carrie would arrive. He still couldn't quite believe she was really into the plan they'd come up with. He was definitely eager to see if it worked the way he wanted.

He'd never really noticed Carrie before. Oh, he'd run into her at different places in town, but he'd never really *noticed* her like he had when she'd stopped by yesterday. He wasn't sure why.

She'd looked so pretty, with her dark hair loose around her shoulders and wearing a pink blouse and jeans that revealed a slender waist, slim hips and medium-size breasts. She had a heart-shaped face with beautiful violet-blue eyes and lush lips that looked very kissable.

He wondered if he would have found her as attractive if she hadn't offered to help him expose his father's murderer. Still, it didn't matter if he found her wildly attractive or not—there was absolutely no room in his heart for anything resembling romance.

The only thing that burned in his heart was the absolute need for revenge. He had to catch his father's killer to somehow prove to Big John that he'd been worthy of his love. But that wasn't a thought he explored too deeply. He just wanted his father's killer behind bars.

It was a few minutes after four when a knock fell on his door. He answered to see his brother Johnny and his fiancée, Chelsea Black, standing on his porch. It hadn't been that long ago that Chelsea's best friend had tried to kill her. Thankfully she hadn't succeeded, and Chelsea was safe and sound today, with her "friend" awaiting trial for attempted murder.

"Hey, we were just going to the big house for dinner and were wondering if you were coming, too," Johnny now said.

Since their father's death, whenever possible the siblings tried to eat dinner with their mother. But lately Luke hadn't been going. It ticked him off too badly to sit and eat at the long dining table, staring at the empty chair where his father used to sit.

"Luke, come with us," Chelsea urged. "It's been a while since you've eaten with all of us, and it would make your mom happy if you came."

Chelsea's mother, Stella Black, owned the ranch next to the Kings'. Chelsea had always seemed like a younger sister to Luke, and very soon she was going to officially be his sister-in-law. She already lived with Johnny, and they had loved each other forever. They were engaged but hadn't set a wedding date yet.

When John King had been murdered, Chelsea's mother had thrown her hat into the mayoral ring, running on the same platform Luke's father had run on. Last week Stella had won the election and was now the newly elected mayor of the small town of Coyote Creek.

"Tell her I'm sorry, but I can't tonight," Luke said. "I have a guest coming by soon, and she and I have plans to hang out together."

One of Johnny's dark brows rose. "She? She who?"

"Carrie Carlson," Luke replied. "She came out here yesterday to see how I was getting along, and one thing led to another and I asked her to come hang out and then later to go to the Red Barn with me."

"From what I hear, she's a nice person," Johnny said.

"Yes, she is," Chelsea added. "She's come into

Ashley's store before. Just don't go breaking her heart."

"That's certainly not my intention," Luke replied with a dry laugh.

"That's never your intention, but you've left a trail of broken hearts behind you," Chelsea said chidingly.

Luke wanted to tell them it wasn't like that between him and Carrie. They were merely partners, not potential lovers, but he couldn't very well say that and keep his cover. Johnny would give him absolute hell if he knew what Luke was doing, and Luke wasn't in the head space to hear another lecture from his older brother.

"Anyway, tell Mom I said hi and I'll see her sometime tomorrow," Luke said.

He breathed a sigh of relief when they left. He didn't appreciate Chelsea making it sound like he broke hearts on purpose. He never intentionally meant to hurt any woman. He usually went out with a woman several times, and if no real spark happened with her, he then moved on. What else was he supposed to do? But all that was in his past now. He would be "dating" Carrie now, but it was only for pretend. This evening, with Carrie's help, he would truly begin his quest to get his father's murderer once and for all.

At five, Luke took a hot shower, wincing as the water sprayed against his bruised ribs. After showering he changed into a clean pair of jeans and a royal blue polo shirt. He slapped on some cologne and then stared at himself in the mirror over the sink.

The bruise on his chin was beginning to turn an ugly light purple and yellow, but at least that meant it was healing. Still, it ticked him off every time he saw it. It had been such an unfair fight. He turned away from the mirror and returned to his recliner to wait for Carrie.

At precisely six o'clock a knock sounded on the door. Luke got up to answer, but before he did, a wave of nervousness tightened his gut. Was this a stupid idea? The last thing he wanted to do was put Carrie in any kind of danger. But what kind of danger could occur with them just having a drink at the Red Barn?

Before he could change his mind, he opened the door. "Hi, Carrie." She looked pretty in tight jeans and a purple blouse that hugged her body and turned her blue eyes to a deep, beautiful violet.

"Hi, Lucas." She offered him a warm smile.

He stepped out on the porch with her. "You look really nice."

"Thanks, so do you," she replied.

"Thanks right back. I thought maybe I'd show you around the place, maybe introduce you to my brothers if we run into them."

"That sounds great," she said agreeably.

They left the porch and began walking side by side up the lane that led to most all the other buildings on the property. "Did you have a good day?" she asked.

"It was all right," he replied. "I've definitely learned over the last few days that I'm not a man who likes to sit around and do nothing."

She flashed him another bright smile. "Luke, you weren't sitting around and doing nothing. You were healing, and that takes a lot of work."

He laughed. "It sure didn't feel like a lot of work." An awkward silence ensued as they continued up the lane. "Uh...nice evening," he finally said. The air still retained the warmth of the day and smelled of green grass and the various wildflowers that grew along the side of the lane.

"It's a beautiful evening," she agreed. "Early summer is absolutely my favorite time of year. I love seeing everything come alive after winter. I love the warm days and cool nights. What about you? What season do you like most?"

He frowned thoughtfully. "Definitely fall for me. I love the leaves all turning different colors. I like cool nights when I can burn a fire in my fireplace." He laughed. "I don't think anyone has ever asked me what season I like before."

"Then you must be hanging out with the wrong crowd," she said with a teasing grin.

"Maybe so," he replied. "This is my brother

Johnny's place," he said as they approached the next house. "I'd introduce you to him, but he and his fiancée, Chelsea Black, are at the big house eating dinner. I'll take you to the barn and we might find Caleb there. He's living in one of the rooms set up for our ranch hands, and he rarely goes to dinner with the family."

"I've seen him around town before, but I've never been introduced to him. I know you want me to try to make friends with him, so meeting him is an important first step in the process."

"He can be…uh…strange sometimes," Luke replied. Luke knew his brother was drinking too much and was smoking weed. However, he didn't know what else his brother might be doing or taking, and that worried him.

"That's okay. Everyone can be a bit strange at times," she replied.

So far, he was finding Carrie remarkably easy to get along with, which was good, since he was planning on spending a lot of time with her.

"Wasn't today your first day of vacation?" he asked, remembering something she'd said the evening before.

"It was," she replied as they headed toward the large barn in the distance.

"What did you do to celebrate?"

"The first thing I did was slept in sinfully late, and then I cooked myself a good breakfast. I then beelined for the sofa and watched television for most of the afternoon. I'll admit it was a lazy, completely unproductive day."

Luke laughed. "So, we both had relatively unproductive days today."

They reached the barn and walked inside. To the left were hay bales stacked almost to the ceiling. To the right was a wooden staircase leading up to the second floor, where the other rooms for the ranch hands were located, and immediately in front of them was a wooden door.

"Caleb is living here right now," he said and then knocked on the door.

To his surprise, Caleb answered almost immediately. "Hey, Luke. What's up?" He was clad in jeans and a white T-shirt that was spattered with paint in a variety of colors, and his long black hair, tied back at the nape of his neck, looked like it could use a good washing.

Luke was grateful that although Caleb smelled like beer, he didn't appear to be drunk or high... yet. "I thought I'd stop by to introduce you to my new friend Carrie Carlson."

"Hi, Caleb. It's very nice to meet you," she said.

"Yeah, nice to meet you, too," Caleb replied.

"I hear you're an artist. Do you paint in oils?" she asked.

Caleb's pale blue eyes lit up a bit, and he looked at her with more interest. "Yeah, definitely in oils."

"What about watercolors? Do you ever paint with them?" she asked.

"Nah, watercolors are for artists who want to paint in vague, nebulous colors and figures. I like the boldness of oil much better." He looked at her curiously. "Are you an artist, too?"

"Oh no, nothing like that," she said with a laugh. "But I do like art. I'd love to see some of your work sometime."

Caleb frowned. "I don't know about that. I'm not ready for him or Johnny to see my work yet." He pointed a finger at Luke.

Carrie laughed again. "Caleb, I don't have to share with them what you share with me. Anyway, I'm just putting it out there that I would love to see your work."

Caleb stared at her for a long moment. "I'll think about it," he finally said.

"Well, it was nice to meet you," Carrie said.

"You'll be seeing a lot of her around here," Luke said, and he reached out to hold Carrie's hand. Her fingers were warm, her skin surprisingly soft, and even as they walked away from the barn, he found himself oddly reluctant to let go.

"How did I do?" she asked softly once they had walked onward from the barn.

"You did excellent," he replied. "You didn't push him too hard, and that bit about not sharing with me whatever he shares with you was perfect."

They turned around and headed back toward his place. "So, I threw out some bait—let's just hope he takes it," Carrie said. "Hopefully not only will he show me his paintings, but with time he'll confide in me about his feelings and dealings with your father."

"And now we move on to the next phase of our operation," he said, finally releasing her hand as they reached his place. "In about an hour or so we'll head to the Red Barn, and hopefully Jeffries will be there, too."

Luke's heart clenched tight as he thought of the man he believed killed his father. Thanks to Carrie, for the first time since his father's murder, he believed he had a real shot at overhearing Jeffries saying something incriminating.

And it didn't hurt that Carrie was pleasing to the eyes and easy to talk to. So far this felt like a partnership made in heaven, but if there was anything Luke had learned over the past couple of months, it was that hopes and plans and dreams could be stolen away in the blink of an eye…in two shots from a gun. And heaven could quickly become a horrifying hell.

CARRIE HAD ALWAYS fantasized about spending time with Luke. Now her fantasies were coming true, but with one difference. In her fantasies he had desperately wanted to spend time with her; in her dreams he'd been totally smitten with her.

She was acutely aware right now that the only reason he was spending time with her was with the hopes of catching his father's killer. He saw her as a partner in his quest, but he certainly didn't see her as a desirable woman he wanted in his life…yet.

But to be honest, she wasn't sure if she really wanted to be desired by him. Certainly, she'd entertained thoughts of lust where he was concerned in the past, but her thoughts had been based solely on a kind of schoolgirl crush.

She would have to get to know him better, although right now it was so far, so good. Her body had even tingled when he'd taken hold of her hand, even though she knew he was only playing a role of pretend boyfriend.

After being introduced to Caleb, they had returned to Luke's place and talked about their plans for the night. Luke knew Peter Jeffries drove a dark blue pickup truck, and he also knew the plate number.

At eight o'clock they got into Luke's truck to head to the Red Barn. "If Jeffries is already there, then we go inside and get the closest table we can to his," Luke said. "And if he isn't there, then we wait in the truck until he gets there."

"Sounds like a good plan to me," she replied. "I

know he seems to be at the Red Barn almost every night. At least, he's always been there when I've gone there with friends."

"I still can't believe you're doing this for me, Carrie." He cast her a quick sideways glance. "I'll never be able to thank you enough."

"You don't have to thank me. I'm just glad I can help you in this way." Darkness had fallen outside, making it more difficult for her to see his features.

"I… I've just felt pretty alone in all this. Nobody else feels the driving need that I feel to put my father's killer behind bars. It eats at me all the time. I can't think of anything else. Johnny keeps telling me to let it go, to wait for Lane to do his job, but I've been waiting for that and nothing has happened."

She saw his hands tighten on the steering wheel. "Sorry, I didn't mean to go off like that," he said.

"Don't apologize for speaking your feelings," she replied. She reached out and touched his forearm. "I hope this works, Luke. I really hope you get what you need and can find some peace."

"I won't have any peace as long as the killer is out there walking free," he replied. "He needs to pay for what he did. It's important I do this for my dad, to prove…" He let his voice drift off, making her wonder what he needed to prove—and to whom.

The moon was bright overhead as he pulled into

the parking lot of the Red Barn. The lot was lit with several lights, and even though it was a week-night, it was half-filled with vehicles, including Peter Jeffries's pickup truck.

The bar/dance hall was housed in a large, bright red barnlike structure. Neon signs advertising various brews flashed from all the windows. Luke threw an arm around her shoulders as they headed for the front door.

Oh, he smelled so good, and she fit so neatly against his side. The thought flittered through her head but was quickly replaced by the soberness of what they wanted to accomplish.

Luke dropped his arm from around her as they walked into the bar. Peanut shells crunched underfoot, and the air was heavy with the scents of booze, greasy bar food and a combination of different colognes and perfumes, with an underlying touch of perspiration.

The music from overhead wasn't as loud as it usually was on the weekends. Still, several couples were on the dance floor, dancing to the country-western tune that played.

Peter and several other men sat at a round table near the dance floor. Thankfully there was an empty two-top right next to where they sat. She and Luke made their way to that table.

"Whoa, look who it is…the loser Luke King," Peter said, and the other three men at his table laughed as if he'd said something particularly brilliant.

Peter was a thin man with short, dark hair and equally dark eyes. He had a wide forehead, a small nose and lips that were usually turned up in a sneer. Every time Carrie and her friends came here, Peter and his band of creeps sniffed around them like dogs in heat. As far as Carrie was concerned, they were all disgusting.

"Hey, I'm not looking for any trouble here. I just want to enjoy a few drinks with Carrie," Luke replied evenly.

"Knock yourself out, lover boy," Peter said. Luke took the chair facing their table, and Carrie took the seat with her back to the men. "Or maybe you'd prefer if we knocked you out," Peter added. Once again, the rest of the men at his table all guffawed.

"I'd like to punch him in his smug little face," Luke said, his voice a low burn of barely suppressed rage.

"That won't accomplish what you want," she replied. "Luke." She reached out and touched his hand, hoping to reach him through his obvious anger.

He visibly drew in a deep breath. "What can I get you to drink?" he finally asked, his voice more even and measured.

"A beer is fine."

He raised one of his dark brows. "Are you sure? I would have pegged you as a froufrou kind of drinker."

She laughed. "You must have me confused with somebody else. I'm just a down-home kind of girl who enjoys a cold beer now and then."

"Then the woman shall have a beer. I'll be right back." He got up from the table and headed for the bar located against the back wall.

The minute he left, Carrie leaned back to see if she could catch any of the conversation at Peter's table. It was fairly easy to hear them. She knew from other nights that the drunker Peter got, the louder he became.

Right now, they were talking about women. They disgusted her with their sexist, filthy words about various women and their body parts. They were boasting about their conquests and whom they wanted to "nail" next. They were definitely all repulsive.

She watched Luke coming back to the table through the small crowd. Even if they weren't romantic partners, she hoped he got what he needed to get to a place of peace.

As a nurse, Carrie knew just how bad it was to stress and harbor the kind of anger, the kind of rage that radiated out from Luke. She'd seen first-hand how negatively those kinds of emotions could affect the entire body, and that's the last thing she would wish on anybody.

Still, she couldn't help but notice how utterly hunky he looked tonight. The royal blue polo did amazing things to his eyes. With his rich black hair and those beautiful eyes, he was definitely a piece of eye candy.

He sat back at the table, placed a beer in front of her and then leaned closer to her. "Anything interesting?" he asked.

"Not a thing," she replied.

"I didn't even ask you if you wanted something from the kitchen. Would you like something?"

"No, thanks." She took a sip of her beer and smiled at him. "I'm good for now."

He moved his chair so he was no longer sitting across from her but rather next to her. It would allow him to better hear the conversations going on at the other table.

"So, how did you get into nursing?" he asked.

"When I was thirteen, my mother was diagnosed with stage-four liver cancer. My father and I spent a lot of time in the hospital with her before she finally passed away. I saw how caring the nurses were toward my mother, how patient and kind they were to me and my dad. I knew immediately that I wanted to be one of those caring nurses for other people."

"I'm sorry. I didn't know about your mother," he said.

She shrugged. "There's no reason you should have known. Anyway, that's why I became a nurse. I have a genuine desire to help people who are ill."

"You were so young to lose your mother," he said.

She nodded. "For the first year after she was gone, I felt utterly lost without her." For just a moment she remembered the grief, the despair she had gone through when her mother passed away. "Thankfully I had a warm, loving father to help me through my grief."

"Is your father still alive?" Luke asked.

"He is." She smiled at thoughts of her father, who was her biggest cheerleader and advocate in life. "He works as a medical equipment salesman and travels the four-state area."

"Do you live at home with him?" he asked.

"No, I rent a house in town with Emily Timmons. Do you know her?" she asked.

"She's a nurse, too, right?"

"Right," Carrie replied.

"Yeah, I've seen her around town, but I don't really know her," he replied.

"She works in Dr. Morris's office and I work in Dr. Holloway's office, and we both work at the hospital whenever we get called in. We get along great, and she's an awesome roommate."

"That's nice," he replied.

They sipped their beers in silence for several moments, both of them listening to the conversation at the table behind them. The men were now talking about their work on the Bridges ranch.

"What do you like to do in your spare time?" Luke asked. She understood other women's attraction to Luke. Aside from his obvious physical attributes, when he gazed at her so intently, he made her feel as if she was the single most important person in the entire world. It was a heady quality for a man to possess.

There was no question he had a reputation as a heartbreaker. Carrie wasn't looking to get her heart broken by him. True, she'd entertained a crush on him for a while, but really, she just wanted to get to know him better.

"Carrie?"

Her face warmed as she realized she'd been staring at him and deep in her own thoughts. "I like riding horseback and having picnics. I enjoy reading and watching mysteries on television." She smiled. "And I also enjoy checking up with former patients to see how they're getting along."

He grinned at her. "Thank goodness for that last part. So, do you own a horse?"

"Sadly, no. When I want to ride, I go to Dickerson's ranch and rent one of his horses for an hour or two," she replied.

"Dickerson only owns a bunch of poor old nags. You'll have to come out one day and ride one of our horses. We've got a couple of good, sweet-natured ones."

"I'd love that," she replied.

"Then we'll definitely plan a day for that," he replied.

To her dismay, Peter and his friends got up from their table and headed for the exit. Luke watched them go with darkened eyes. "Well, this was a bust," he said.

"Luke, I have a feeling this is going to be more of a marathon than a sprint," she replied.

He sighed. "Yeah, I know. I was just hoping…" His voice trailed off.

"We'll catch him on another night," she said. "If he really fired the gun that killed your father, then eventually I believe he will get drunk enough, stupid enough to say something about it, and we'll be here to hear him."

"You're right. At least now we can relax and enjoy the last of our beers." She felt some of his tension ebb away.

"So, what do you enjoy doing in your spare time?" she asked.

"Lately I haven't enjoyed doing much of anything." He took a drink of his beer and then continued, "I used to enjoy a leisurely ride through the pastures in the evenings. I also like to do a little fishing in the pond next to my place. There are some fairly big catfish and crappie in there."

"That sounds like fun," she said, thinking about sitting next to him on the wooden dock she'd seen extending out over the pond. The sun would be warm on their shoulders, and his attractive scent would wrap around her.

"Most of the women in town don't think fishing is much fun," he said.

"And you would know that because you've dated most of the women in town," she said teasingly.

He looked at her in surprise and then laughed. "Okay, I'll admit I've dated quite a bit. What about you? What's your dating history?"

"I dated Rory Howard for a while, but we broke up a little over a year ago."

"I know him. He seems like a nice guy. Why did the two of you break up?" Luke asked.

"We wanted different things in life. Eventually I want a family, and Rory didn't know if he wanted children. He was still big on partying and hanging out with his friends. Anyway, the breakup was amicable. Since then, I've dated a few other guys, but nobody seriously."

"So, I'm not taking you away from any other man right now," he said.

She laughed. "Definitely not. If I had a boyfriend, I wouldn't have agreed to all of this." She took the last drink of her beer.

"And I'm still very grateful to you." He drained the last of his bottle of beer. "Are you ready to get out of here?"

"Ready when you are," she replied. It wasn't like this was a real date, where they might enjoy a second drink or hit the dance floor. The reason they were here had left, so there was really no reason for them to remain.

"Then let's call it a night." He stood from the table, and she did as well.

He took her arm and led her toward the exit. She liked him. Even though it was obvious he held a lot of anger inside him, he had said and done nothing to change the little crush she had on him.

They had just stepped out into the cool night air when the boom of a gun split the air. A bullet whizzed by within inches of her head, and then she was thrown to the ground with Luke's body on top of her.

Chapter Three

Another boom sounded, and the bullet pinged precariously close to them. "Stay down," he shouted to Carrie, who wiggled frantically beneath him. Luke's gaze shot all around, trying to identify the location of the shooter.

What in the hell was going on? Dammit, he hadn't even worn his gun tonight. Whom was the shooter aiming at? Carrie? Him? Anybody? A frightened cry came from Carrie, and still he remained covering her, waiting for another shot to come.

Every muscle in his body screamed with tension. Adrenaline filled his veins, and he drew deep breaths in an effort to slow the frantic beat of his heart.

People from the bar began coming outside to see what was going on. "Get back inside," Luke yelled at them, not wanting anyone to get hurt.

"Take cover and call Chief Caldwell. It's an active shooter."

Thankfully the others quickly went back into the safety of the bar. There was a squeal of tires in the far left of the parking lot. Luke tried to see the vehicle, but it was gone before he could get a visual on it.

Seconds ticked by…slow seconds that turned into minutes. The silence became deafening as he waited to see if any more bullets would fly, but he had a feeling the vehicle he'd heard peeling away had been the shooter fleeing the scene.

It was only when he heard the sounds of sirens in the distance that he relaxed a bit. He got to his knees and waited. Nothing happened. No more shots fired. He finally got to his feet as Lane's patrol car and two others squealed into the parking lot. It was only then that he helped Carrie to her feet.

She slammed into his body, wrapped her arms tightly around his neck and buried her face in his shirt as she shivered and cried.

Luke held her close, knowing that she must have been terrified. Even with everything going on around them, he was vaguely aware of how nicely she fit against him and how wonderful she smelled.

She finally pulled away from him. "I'm sorry,"

she said as she swiped at her tears. "I'm... I'm so sorry."

"What are you sorry about?" he asked.

"I... I didn't mean to break down."

"It's okay, Carrie," he assured her.

By that time Lane had approached them as three other officers fanned out in the parking lot with their weapons drawn. "I got a call of an active shooter," Lane said and motioned for the two of them to get back inside the bar.

Once inside, he yelled to get everyone's attention. The music halted, and a silence fell over the room. "Nobody leaves this building until I tell you it's okay." He then turned to Luke and Carrie. "Tell me what happened?"

"Carrie and I walked out the door to leave, and somebody shot at us," Luke said. "There were two shots and they seemed to be coming from the left area of the parking lot."

"Did you see the shooter?"

Luke shook his head. "No. After the first shot, we hit the ground."

"And then...then the person shot at us again," Carrie added, her voice trembling. Luke threw an arm around her shoulder and pulled her closer for comfort. He hated that he'd put her in this kind of danger. But damned if he could have foreseen somebody shooting at them the minute they stepped outside.

"There were two shots and then it stopped," Luke said. "And then I heard a vehicle squealing out of the parking lot. I don't think the shooter is around here anymore."

Lane looked directly at him. "So, who have you ticked off now?"

"Nobody," Luke replied irritably. "I've spent the last couple of days in my cabin all alone. Tonight, I invited Carrie out for a drink, and unless she has an overly protective brother who likes to shoot at her boyfriends, I haven't done anything to anyone."

"We just had a beer and decided to leave and go back to Luke's place," Carrie said, her voice a little stronger now. She moved out from under Luke's arm. "And I don't have a big brother and Luke did nothing wrong. In fact, he protected me by throwing himself over me."

"Do you think you were the specific target, or was the perp looking to shoot anyone who walked out the door?" Lane asked.

"There's no way to know," Luke replied. "But nobody should have a reason to shoot at me."

"Or me," Carrie added.

One of the officers came in the door. "We've swept the parking lot and didn't find anyone," he said.

"And you didn't get a glimpse of the vehicle you heard pull away?" Lane asked Luke.

"Sorry, I didn't. I was too busy trying not to get shot," Luke replied dryly.

Lane raked a hand over his thinning brown hair, his pale blue eyes troubled. "Let's hope this was just an isolated incident. Somebody got liquored up and decided to shoot randomly." He frowned. "There are too damn many people owning guns these days."

"Yeah, well, starting tomorrow there will be one more person with a gun," Luke replied. "From now on I'm not leaving my house without my weapon."

Lane turned back to the officer. "Do one more sweep of the area and then I'll start letting people go."

"There's a small group of people who have arrived since we've been here, and they are waiting to come inside. Right now, we've got them all sitting in their vehicles and waiting until you give us the go-ahead," the officer replied.

"One more sweep and then we'll be done here," Lane replied. "Is there anything else you can tell me about the shooting?" Lane asked Luke when the officer left.

Luke frowned thoughtfully. "Everything happened so fast. I can't think of anything else."

"What about you, Carrie?" Lane asked.

"I can't tell you anything except that I've never been so terrified in my entire life," she replied.

She wrapped her arms around herself as if fighting against an inner chill.

A long forty-five minutes later, Luke and Carrie were in his truck heading back to his place. "At least you know I provide an exciting time on a first date," Luke said.

Carrie gave a small laugh. "Definitely almost too exciting for me."

"I'm so sorry, Carrie," he said.

"There's nothing for you to apologize for," she replied.

"If I hadn't brought you there, then you wouldn't have had to go through all this," he replied. Now that it was all over guilt weighed down on him. Thank God Carrie hadn't been hurt.

"Let yourself off the hook, Luke. I chose to be there. You didn't kidnap me and force me to go to the Red Barn with you. You aren't responsible for anything. I've gone to the Red Barn plenty of times without you. This could have happened on any one of those nights."

He shot her a quick glance. Her pretty features were illuminated by the soft light from the dashboard. "You're a nice woman, Carrie."

She released another small laugh. "I am pretty easygoing. I only get angry about things that really matter. Being shot at falls in the category of scaring me half to death."

"It scared me half to death, too," he admitted.

He turned into the long lane that would take them to his house at the end. "Why don't you come in for a little while?" he said as he parked in front of his place.

"Okay. I'm definitely not ready to go home and go right to bed. I still have too much adrenaline rushing around in my head and body."

"I hear that," Luke agreed. He parked his truck, and together they got out. He unlocked the door and ushered her inside.

"Have a seat," he said and gestured to the sofa. "Do you want something to drink?"

"No, I'm good," she replied and sank down on the thick cushions.

He sat down in his recliner facing her. "Do you think it's possible Peter waited for us to walk out and then shot at us?"

A tiny frown danced into her forehead. "No," she answered immediately. "First of all, there was no ill will between you and him when they left the bar. And from what I've heard about Peter's shooting skills, if it was him, he wouldn't have missed the shot."

"Peter's shooting skills are what put him on the very top of my suspect list," Luke replied, his stomach tightening at the mere mention of the man's name.

"Like Lane said, I'm leaning toward it being somebody drunk and reckless."

"Drunk and stupid," Luke added. "At least you survived your first date with me." He grinned at her, hoping to lighten the mood.

She laughed. She had a nice laugh. It was light and musical and easy on the ears. "I survived thanks to you protecting me." Her gaze was warm on him. "Thank you, Luke, for throwing me down and using yourself as a shield to protect me. That's real hero material as far as I'm concerned."

"Hell, Carrie. I'm no hero. I'm just a man on a mission to find my father's killer."

"Peter and his gang of misfits didn't stay long tonight. There will be another night where they'll stay longer and get drunker, and maybe then Peter will boast about what he's done," Carrie replied. "If he's a guilty man, then eventually we'll get him, Luke."

He liked the *we* in her sentence. For the past two months, since his father's death, Luke had felt so all alone. None of his family members seemed to feel the real burn for justice that Luke felt. Now he had somebody who seemed to understand him, who wanted to help him, and it felt good.

"I think it's time I get home," she now said and stood. Luke got out of his chair. Together they walked to his front door. "Same place, same time tomorrow?" she asked.

"Are you sure you're still in this after what happened tonight?"

"Definitely," she replied without hesitation. "As far as I'm concerned, what happened tonight was just a fluke—a drunk with a gun. I'm very much still in this."

She looked so determined, with her violet eyes shining brightly. Luke could smell the scent of her, that flowers-and-spice fragrance that he found wildly attractive.

For a brief moment, he wanted to kiss her. She looked so pretty and so damned kissable. They stood so close to each other that he could feel her body heat. He must have leaned forward, for her lips parted slightly as if in open invitation.

Kiss her, a little voice whispered inside him. He snapped back, ignored the inner voice and broke the crazy moment. The last thing he wanted to do was give her the wrong idea about their partnership.

"How about I pick you up at your place tomorrow evening?" he said and took a step back from her.

"That would be fine. Shall I text you my address?"

"Yeah, we should exchange phone numbers." They both took out their phones and took care of that issue.

"Okay, then I'll text you sometime tomorrow and we can finalize the plans for tomorrow night." She smiled. "Good night, Luke."

"Good night, Carrie. Drive safely." He watched as she got into her car and then headed up the lane. Once her taillights disappeared from his view, he went back into his house and returned to the recliner.

He thought about that moment when he'd wanted to kiss Carrie. It had definitely been a wild impulse. It had to be because he knew she was on his side and they had just gone through a frightening experience together. It had nothing to do with any real desire for her, he told himself. He had no time or energy for desire. He wanted nothing to do with romance.

Carrie was a partner, and she would never be anything more. He would forever be grateful to her if their plan worked and they caught Peter confessing that he'd killed Big John King.

Of course, Carrie hadn't said or done anything that would make him believe she was romantically interested in him. Thankfully they were both on the same page—she probably wouldn't have wanted a kiss from him anyway.

Now all he could hope was that the plan worked and they caught Peter saying something incriminating. Only that would ease the grief, the all-consuming rage that ate at him day and night.

EVEN THOUGH CARRIE was officially on vacation, she got a call early the next morning from Dr. Holloway begging her to come into the office. Two of the other nurses had called in sick, and he had a full schedule. He told her he desperately needed her help.

Although she had been exhausted from all the events of the night before, she'd come in to work. It had been a crazy, busy day in the office, but thankfully at five o'clock it was done.

She was in the small break room getting her things together to leave to go home when Dr. James Holloway walked in. He was a short man with thin brown hair, a slightly oversize nose and pale blue eyes.

Carrie knew he was thirty-nine years old, and he was a good doctor with a thriving practice. He also had a three-year-old little boy that he was raising from a previous relationship.

"Carrie, I can't thank you enough for coming in last-minute today," he now said to her.

"It wasn't a problem," she replied. She grabbed her purse from the locker that was assigned to her, hoping he would just go away.

Far too often her boss stood closer to her than was necessary, or he'd reach across her and brush against her breasts. She never knew if it was truly an accident or on purpose. What she did know was that he often made her feel very uncomfortable.

"I miss you when you aren't here in the office, Carrie," he said, immediately making her feel that discomfort again. He often teetered on the line of professionalism with her.

"Carrie, would you consider going out with me for a drink this evening?"

Every muscle in her body tensed. "I'm sorry, Dr. Holloway, I already have plans for this evening. I've been seeing Luke King, and in any case, I'm sure I've mentioned before that I don't believe in mixing business with pleasure."

His blue eyes narrowed. "I'm a much better fit for you than some dumb rancher. Carrie, you're way too smart for somebody like Luke King. You need a mature man like me."

"In any case, I'm seeing Luke this evening, and I'm ready to leave now." He stood between her and the exit, but thankfully after a moment of staring at her, he moved aside. "Good night, Dr. Holloway. I'll see you when I get back from vacation."

She didn't breathe until she reached her car in the parking lot. She'd known for some time that he had a thing for her. The other nurses teased her about the crush their boss had on her. But this was the first time he'd taken it a step further and had asked her out. It had validated all those times when she'd believed he wasn't just "accidentally" touching her. Tonight, he'd gone way over the line.

He was a creep, and maybe it was time she looked for another job. Her boss had been making her uncomfortable for some time, but in a small town like Coyote Creek, jobs weren't exactly a dime a dozen. Still, the idea of going back into that office was repugnant to her.

She shoved these thoughts out of her mind and focused on the night ahead. She was going to have to hurry to get home and then get ready for Luke to pick her up at six thirty.

Luke. She couldn't help but feel a pull toward him. He was nice and could be quite charming. He seemed genuinely interested in getting to know her, and there had been a moment the night before when she'd thought he was going to kiss her.

She'd seen a flash of desire in his eyes. He'd moved in intimately close to her, and her heart had quickened with sweet anticipation. And then he'd stepped back and the moment had been lost.

Despite the shooting at the Red Barn last night, she wasn't afraid to go back there tonight. She'd thought about the shooting long after she'd gotten home the night before. She did not believe she and Luke had been the specific targets. She did believe, whomever the shooter was, he would have fired those shots toward whoever stepped out the door.

Besides, she wanted to be there for Luke. Aside from the fact that she liked him, she'd seen flashes of the pain he held inside, and she'd felt the grief that still clung to him. If anyone needed a friend, it was Luke.

It took her only minutes to get from the doctor's office to the attractive two-story house just off Main Street that she shared with Emily.

The house was painted a light gray with darker gray shutters. The street was lined with tall, mature trees, and a huge oak stood in their front yard. She pulled into the driveway next to Emily's car and got out.

"Hello," she called out as she stepped into the living room.

"In the kitchen," Emily yelled back.

The living room was decorated in a mishmash kind of style. Emily had brought with her a slightly broken-down, overstuffed beige sofa from her parents' basement, and Carrie had added a black and glass coffee table and matching end tables she'd bought at a garage sale.

The two women had pooled their money to buy a nice brown chair for the living room and a dining room table, dishes and pots and pans. Each of them had brought their own bedroom furniture, and for the last two years they had been good friends and great roommates.

Carrie walked into the kitchen, where Emily sat at the table with a sandwich and chips in front of her. She was clad in a pair of pink scrubs that complemented her light brown hair and pretty hazel eyes.

"Hey, girl," Emily greeted her. "How was your day?"

"It was fine until the end." Carrie went to the refrigerator and pulled out the sandwich meat and a piece of cheese.

"What happened at the end?" Emily asked curiously.

As Carrie made herself a sandwich, she told Emily about Dr. Holloway asking her out for a drink. "Oh, ick," Emily said when Carrie was finished.

"That's what I thought," Carrie said as she finished making her sandwich and sat in the chair opposite Emily.

"You said before that you thought he had a crush on you," Emily said.

"Yeah. I'd often feel him staring at me, and he often invaded my personal space, but he definitely confirmed my suspicions today when he told me I needed a 'mature man' like him." Carrie began to eat, watching the clock and knowing she still wanted to shower and clean up before Luke arrived.

"That's so disgusting. So, what are you going to do?" Emily asked. "Don't you think things are going to be really awkward now for you at work?"

"Definitely. In fact, things have been awkward there for quite some time now. Is Dr. Morris hiring?" she asked half-kiddingly.

"Actually, he is hiring. Sarah Benson just quit to be a stay-at-home mom." Emily grinned. "Just think of all the fun trouble we could get in working together."

Carrie laughed. "Maybe I'll put in an application with him while I'm on vacation."

"Seriously, I'd love working with you at Dr. Morris's office," Emily said. "He's a really nice man and treats all of us with respect."

"I'd like that, but right now, I need to choke down my sandwich and get upstairs to shower and change. Luke is picking me up at six thirty."

"How's that going?" Emily asked.

"Good. He really seems to be a nice guy, and I'm enjoying spending time with him."

"I wish Lane could find the person who killed Big John. I've heard that the whole King family is still grieving deeply," Emily said. "I feel so sorry for them all. And now I'll shut up and get out of here so you can finish eating."

Emily put her plate in the dishwasher. "I'll talk to you later," she said and then left the kitchen.

The two rarely cooked on the days they both worked. Sandwiches and frozen meals were their best friends on those days. When one of them had a day off, that person usually cooked a real meal for them both.

Carrie finished her sandwich and then headed upstairs to her bedroom. She had the master bedroom that had its own bathroom. She paid a little more rent than Emily did for the privilege. She took off the scrubs she'd worn all day, threw them into a laundry basket and then got into the shower.

As the warm water pelted her, she stifled a couple of yawns. Last night had been a fairly late night and she'd definitely been up and running very early that morning, leaving her a little tired now. However, thoughts of spending more time with Luke shot a welcomed rivulet of much-needed adrenaline through her.

She had no idea if he intended on taking her back to the King ranch to hang out before they went to the Red Barn or not. Six thirty was a bit early to head to the bar, but it was Luke's choice what they did. She was just along for the ride.

Once she was out of the shower, she pulled on a pair of jeans and a long-sleeved spring-green blouse that hugged her body in all the right places. She applied her makeup and then spritzed herself with her favorite perfume.

She was ready with fifteen minutes to spare. She went back downstairs and sat on the sofa to wait for Luke. A small knot of nerves tightened her chest. She couldn't help but feel a little nervous about seeing Luke again. The crush she had on him had only grown with each and every minute she spent with him.

When his knock fell on the door, she jumped

up, grabbed her purse and then went to answer. As usual, he looked totally hot in jeans and a light blue T-shirt. "Hi, Carrie."

"Hey, Luke. I'm ready to go if you are," she replied. "I just need to yell up to Emily and let her know I'm leaving." As Luke stepped just inside the front door, Carrie went to the foot of the staircase and hollered up to her roommate. "Emily, I'm leaving now. I'll lock the door."

"Okay, thanks, Carrie. See you tomorrow," Emily yelled back.

Carrie turned back to Luke and smiled. "Now I'm ready." Together she and Luke left the house and headed for his truck parked at the curb.

"This is an attractive neighborhood," he said.

"Yeah, it's nice and peaceful, and we love living here." It was a quiet neighborhood—most of her neighbors were older couples with grown children.

"Your house looked nice from what little I saw of it." They reached his truck, and he opened the passenger door for her.

"It's actually a hodgepodge of styles that screams for an interior decorator, but it's comfortable. I should have invited you in to see it all," she replied as she got into the truck.

"Next time," he said and flashed her the smile that always shot a delicious warmth through her. He closed her door and then walked around the front of the truck to the driver's door.

"You know, I should have invited you to dinner at the café tonight before we headed to the Red Barn," he said as he pulled away from the curb.

"Next time," she replied with a grin.

He laughed. "You look like spring in that green blouse. It looks very nice."

"Thank you. I look like green grass and you look like blue skies," she replied.

"You're right." He headed down the highway. "I thought we'd hang out around the ranch until later."

"Sounds like a plan," she said, echoing his earlier words and making him laugh once again. He had a wonderful laugh, full and deep-bodied, and she loved hearing it.

He asked her about her day, and she told him about going into the office to help out and then her boss asking her out for a drink.

"Are you interested in him?" Luke asked.

"Heavens, no," she replied with disgust. "To be honest, I find him kind of creepy. He's always made me feel pretty uncomfortable. He's always brushing up too close to me or reaching across me and skimming my breasts. I kept telling myself those things were accidents, but today he definitely crossed the line, so I'll be looking for a new job in the next couple of weeks."

She hadn't realized she'd made up her mind to definitely look for another job until this very moment. She deserved better than working in a place that made her feel so uncomfortable and stressed. She deserved better than working for a man who obviously had little respect for her.

"Good for you," he replied. "You deserve much better than that."

"That's what I was just thinking," she replied.

By that time, they had arrived at Luke's place. "There's something I want to show you," he said as they got out of the truck.

She followed him to the front door. He unlocked it and held it open for her to enter the house. Once inside, he locked the door once again, something he hadn't done before. "I… I've been working on something that I want you to see," he said. "It's in my spare bedroom."

"Okay," she replied slowly. She'd never heard anything negative about the way Luke treated women, but inviting her into his spare bedroom seemed strange, and he was acting odd…like he was suddenly very nervous.

"Nobody else has seen what I'm about to show you, and I hope you won't mention it to anyone else," he said, further intriguing her and making her nervous all at the same time.

"Luke…what is it?"

He reached for her hand and pulled her down a short hallway. They passed what appeared to be Luke's master bedroom. She peeked in and saw a king-size bed covered in a navy bedspread. Navy curtains hung at the windows. From the quick glance she got, it looked neat and clean. Then they came to a closed door.

He dropped her hand and opened the door. "Welcome to my nightmare."

She stepped into the room and looked around in stunned surprise. Large whiteboards covered three of the four walls in the room, and on them were notes about his father's murder.

There was a list of suspects, some crossed out, while others were underlined. Every encounter he'd had with Lane was written down with notes to the side.

She'd known Luke was fixated on finding his father's killer, but this spoke to a depth of obsession that could make a person descend into utter madness.

"EAT, BILLIE. You know you have to eat, so open your mouth." He guided the spoon, but just before he could put the food in, the mouth snapped shut.

"Dammit." He threw the bowl of oatmeal across the room. The plastic bowl hit the far kitchen wall and slowly slid down to the floor, leaving a trail of lumpy oatmeal behind.

He got up from the table, too angry to sit for another moment and too angry to clean up the mess he'd just made. He went into the living room and threw himself on the sofa.

It wasn't supposed to be this way. Dammit, it wasn't supposed to be this…this hard. He was supposed to have a partner…a wife to help him. But he'd been cheated.

And soon he'd have to change a dirty diaper, and that would only bring his rage on all over again. It could have been different. It *should* have been different. His stomach clenched and his head ached as the anger continued to build inside him all over again.

That bitch. That snotty nurse—he'd make her pay. He'd tried the other night at the Red Barn. He'd sat in the parking lot and waited, hoping to get off one perfect shot. But he'd missed her, and then that pseudohero Luke King had covered her body with his own.

Now his anger toward her had only increased tenfold. He'd make her pay for what she hadn't done and all the lies she'd told him. He was going to enjoy making her pay—and the ultimate compensation to him for all her lies was her death.

Chapter Four

Luke had been afraid that by showing Carrie his murder boards, he might chase her away. He'd worried that she might think him completely insane and she'd run for the hills as fast as she could.

However, he'd been pleased that she'd not only not run from him, but she'd studied his work and talked to him about other suspects and why he had ultimately discounted or added them.

A week and a half had passed since that night—a week and a half of frustration, as far as the case was concerned. He and Carrie had sat for hours in the Red Barn, listening to Peter and his drunken buddies whoop and holler, laugh and crow. He'd heard them talk about everything but the murder of Big John King.

Luke's frustration, along with his rage, had grown with each day that had passed. That was why he had invited Carrie to come to the ranch for some horseback riding today. He needed something to ease the rage and the pain, if only for a couple of hours.

It was a beautiful Saturday afternoon, and Luke was hoping a little horseback riding would erase some of the pressure, some of the stress that rode his shoulders almost all the time.

The pressure definitely eased somewhat whenever he was with Carrie. It was strange, but spending time with her brought him a peaceful calm that was positively intoxicating.

He'd gotten to know her better with each evening they had spent together. She made him laugh, something he had forgotten to do since his father's death. And, to his surprise over the past week, she and Caleb had become quite friendly as well.

His brother rarely opened up to anyone, yet for some reason he seemed to be open to a friendship with Carrie. As far as Luke was concerned, it only spoke to Carrie's warmth and sweet personality that drew people to her.

He'd introduced her to his mother and his sister, and even Johnny had given Carrie his stamp of approval as a romantic partner for Luke. Of course, they weren't really romantic partners. They were just partners.

As he heard the sound of a car pulling up outside, he stepped out on the porch. He smiled as Carrie parked and then got out.

She looked pretty clad in jeans and a long-sleeved light pink blouse. Her dark brown hair was loose around her shoulders and sparked with red and gold highlights in the bright sunshine.

A swift and strong surge of desire suddenly punched him in the gut. It wasn't the first time he'd experienced it where Carrie was concerned, but it always surprised him when it rose up inside him. It was always unexpected and undesirable.

He just assumed it was because it had been a long time since he'd been with a woman and he and Carrie had been spending a lot of quality time together. Still, it was definitely completely inappropriate. He quickly squashed it down. There was no place for that kind of feeling where Carrie was concerned.

"Are you ready to do some riding today?" he asked as she approached him.

"I can't wait," she replied. Her eyes shone brightly. "As long as you don't intend to put me on the back of some wild bucking bronco, I'll be good."

He laughed. "I promise, no wild bucking bronco. Come on, let's head down to the stables." He grabbed her hand as they walked across the lane from his house and down a path that would eventually lead to more outbuildings. It felt natural to hold her hand even though it was just a ruse to make everyone they encountered think they were in a romantic relationship.

"Did you hear back from Dr. Morris's office yet?" he asked.

"Actually, I heard from him this morning. I start Wednesday morning for him, and I immediately called Dr. Holloway to let him know I wouldn't be working for him anymore."

"How did he take it?"

"I could tell he was pretty ticked off. He was very cool but civil," she replied.

"I'm glad you're getting away from him." Luke's hand tightened around hers. "I didn't like it that your creep boss made you uncomfortable and crossed all kinds of professional lines with you."

"I didn't realize just how uncomfortable I have been until this morning when I got the call from Dr. Morris. I've never felt such a sense of relief as I did when I realized I don't have to go back to work in that place anymore," she replied. "However, I do feel bad that I'm not giving Dr. Holloway two weeks notice."

"You don't owe that man any notice. You don't owe him anything. The minute he brushed up against you, the minute he asked you out, he broke the trust that might warrant him notice," Luke replied firmly.

"Thanks, Luke," she said with a bright smile that shot an explosion of warmth into his stomach. He wasn't sure why her smiles always warmed him, why they always made him feel very special and…happy.

Ahead, the large stables came into view. Luke's rib pain had finally quieted to a mere whisper, and he was looking forward to riding for the first time since his beatdown. He'd wound up taking far more time off than he'd ever intended because his ribs had continued to give him fits.

"I asked one of the ranch hands to get the horses ready for us," he said as they approached the entrance. "The horse I have picked out for you is named Sue. She's a gentle, sweet mare and shouldn't give you any trouble."

"And what's your horse's name?" she asked.

"Storm," he replied. "She's a feisty ride and takes a firm hand, but she trusts me and I trust her."

They stepped across the threshold of the stables. Luke loved the scents of horse and hay and grain. Before his father's death, he'd always loved hanging out in the stables. But the place also held many memories of Big John that now brought a deep grief with them. He hadn't been spending much time out here since his father's murder.

It was here in the stables that he had spent quality time with his father. He and Big John had spent many hours in here talking about the horses and life in general. Luke had cherished those times with his dad.

Hopefully, the grief would eventually pass and he would once again enjoy being in this place with the horses he loved taking care of and being around.

"Hey, Rod," Luke said, greeting the man who stepped out of a nearby stall. "Carrie, this is Rod Jackson, one of the men who help us out around here. Rod, this is Carrie Carlson."

"Hi, Carrie. I've seen you around town before, but it's nice to officially meet you," Rod replied.

"You, too, Rod," she said.

"I've got the horses all saddled up and ready to go," he said to Luke.

"Thanks, Rod. Why don't you bring Sue around and I'll get Storm?" Luke dropped Carrie's hand. "Just wait here," he said to her.

Minutes later they left the stables on their horses and headed out into the pasture. "It feels good to be riding again," he said.

"It feels good to be on a horse that's tall and strong," she replied. She leaned forward and patted Sue's neck. "I'll behave if you behave," she said to her mount.

Luke laughed. "Trust me, she'll behave."

Carrie looked good on the horse. Her posture was perfect, and her hips rolled easily with the horse's gait. As they rode at a leisurely pace, he pointed out the large herd of cattle in the distance and various outbuildings and land features he found interesting.

"That area over there is Caleb's playground," he said, pointing toward a heavily wooded area. His stomach tightened as he thought of his younger brother. When his father had been shot, Caleb's alibi was that he was out in that area taking pictures of various flowers he wanted to paint. But it was an alibi that couldn't be confirmed.

"That field is too full of trees and brush and uneven terrain, so we can't use it as much of anything. Caleb spends a lot of time out in the woods there finding things to photograph and then paint," he added.

"I'll bet it's beautiful," she replied.

"I guess it is. I never go there. Are you ready to do a little galloping?"

"Ready when you are," she replied.

He took off galloping, pleased that she easily kept up with him. The breeze was pleasant on his face, and the sun was warm on his shoulders. Seeing Carrie with her long, dark hair fanning out and her beautiful smile in place as they rode filled him with a pleasure he hadn't felt for a very long time.

As he broke into a full run, her laughter rode the air as she urged Sue to go faster. They raced across the pasture for a short time, and then he reined in and she followed his lead.

"That was exhilarating," she said, and once

again her smile caused a rivulet of warmth to rush through him. "I never get to run like that on Dickerson's horses."

"We'll walk them for a few minutes, and then I've got a place for us to dismount and relax for a little while."

They walked for a few minutes to cool the horses down, and then he led her to a small pond with trees all around and they dismounted. Before she'd arrived, he'd packed a blanket and two soft drinks in his saddlebag. He now spread the blanket out for them to sit on.

"This is nice," she said once they were settled.

"I used to come to this spot a lot to think and just chill."

"It's beautiful here and so peaceful." It was a very peaceful place, with the breeze rustling the leaves overhead and the birds singing their songs from all the trees.

"Yeah, although I have to admit there were times when I came out here to pout," he said.

"Pout? You? You definitely don't seem like the pouting type," she replied with a raise of her perfectly arched, dark eyebrow.

"There was only one thing I ever pouted about." He cast his eyes to the distance, finding it a bit difficult to look at her as he confessed to some of his weakest moments.

"What, Luke? Tell me." She placed her hand on

his forearm in the silent encouragement he'd come to expect from her.

He returned his gaze to her. "I always knew that as the second son, I would come in second when it came to my dad's love, but that was always a hard pill to swallow."

He saw her about to speak, and he held up a hand to stop her. "I know what you're about to say, and I know my father loved me, but Johnny definitely was his go-to son. I'd see them out of horseback together and yearn to be out there with them. Dad depended more on Johnny than he did me. He…he…" Luke broke off, horrified that his emotions had climbed far too close to the surface.

He sucked in several deep breaths to steady himself, mortified by his momentary lack of control. "Anyway, that's what I'd come out here and think about. And now I feel the need to get Dad's killer, to prove to him that I'm the son who loved him more." He released a slightly embarrassed laugh. "Childish, huh?"

"Oh Luke, I'm not about to tell you that your feelings are childish or unwarranted or anything else." She moved closer to him, so close the evocative scent of her eddied in his head. "Your feelings are your feelings. But you must know on some level that your father loved you very much."

"Logically, I know that, but Johnny was a hard act to follow as an older brother. He's always been so sure of himself and his role here at the ranch. He's now pressuring me to get more involved and take charge of a horse-breeding operation here."

"And you don't want to do it?" she asked.

"Yeah, I do want to. It's something my dad wanted to see me do, but I'm just not ready to do it yet."

"Luke, don't put off your life while waiting to catch your father's murderer. I know how badly you want the man responsible behind bars, but life is far too short, and it's okay to find some happiness despite your grief."

He looked into her eyes…her beautiful violet eyes. Without giving it any thought, functioning only on sheer emotion, he leaned forward and captured her lips with his.

CARRIE HAD BEEN waiting for a kiss from Luke for what felt like forever. His lips were wonderfully warm, and she immediately parted hers to invite him to deepen the kiss.

Their tongues danced together in a hot tango as he slowly leaned her back on the blanket. What had begun as a simple kiss quickly turned into something hot and hungry and demanding.

The sound of the birdsongs faded away as she gave herself to the magic of Luke's kiss. Fiery heat flamed through her veins. She was surrounded by the scent of him, a heady scent of sunshine and the woodsy cologne he wore that she loved.

At the moment, if he wanted to strip her naked and make love to her right here, right now, she would welcome it. Over the past week and a half, her feelings for Luke had only deepened. As crazy as it seemed after such a short time, she was definitely on the verge of falling in love with him.

He suddenly released her and shot back up to a sitting position. He raked a hand through his hair and stared down at her, obviously appalled. "God, Carrie... I'm so sorry. That...that shouldn't have happened."

She sat up and held his gaze. "Why? Luke, why shouldn't it have happened? I have been wanting you to kiss me for a while now." She still wanted him to kiss her, to hold her and tell her that he cared for her.

He frowned. "That's not what this partnership is about."

"Don't worry. I haven't lost sight of what our partnership is about, but I like you, Luke. I like you a lot," she confessed.

"And I like you, too, Carrie. But I'm not in a position to have any kind of romantic relationship right now. I thought you understood that."

"I do understand that. I don't expect anything from you. It doesn't matter how many times we kiss. It doesn't even matter if we were to make

love. I still wouldn't expect anything from you."
She thought she saw a flash of desire in the depths
of his eyes, but it was only there only a moment
and then gone.

"I just want to make sure we're both on the same
page," he said. "That's really important to me."

"We are, Luke," she replied fervently in an effort to reassure him. All she could hope for was
that with more time, Luke would realize what they
had between them was something special and romantic and wonderful.

"On that note, why don't we mount up and do
a little more riding?" he said.

Minutes later they were riding once again.
There was no question she was a bit disappointed
by the way their few minutes of passion had
ended. But she knew Luke was single-minded in
his quest. Still, he'd obviously wanted to kiss her
in the first place and that thought shot a river of
delicious warmth through her.

He might believe he had no time or energy for
romance, but emotions couldn't be tamed. They
could only be stuffed down for so long before
they finally had to be acknowledged. If Luke was
falling for her, then eventually he'd have to embrace those feelings. At least that's what she hoped
would happen.

In the meantime, all she could do was continue
to help him pursue Peter's admission of guilt, or

help clear his brother once and for all from being a viable suspect.

They rode for another half an hour and then headed back to the stables. "How about I take you to dinner at the café?" he said once they were walking back toward his house.

"That sounds good. Since I didn't know for sure what the plans would be, I brought a change of clothes. Do you mind if I change and clean up a bit?"

"Not at all," he replied.

"Then I'll just grab my things from my car and meet you in the house."

As Luke headed inside, Carrie grabbed her fresh clothing and a travel cosmetic bag from the back seat of her car, then went into Luke's house.

"I'm going to do a little cleanup before we go, too," he said. "Why don't you use the bathroom in the hallway and I'll use mine in my bedroom."

"Okay," she agreed.

"If you want to take a quick shower, there are towels and washcloths underneath the sink."

Minutes later, Carrie stood beneath a warm shower with her hair pulled into a messy knot on top of her head so as not to get wet.

They had talked about going to the café over the last week but had never actually done it. So, tonight would be the first time they'd be out in public together in a place other than the Red Barn.

Once again, they would be acting like they were a real couple.

It was a fast shower, and then she dressed in a fresh pair of jeans and a long-sleeved royal blue blouse. After applying fresh makeup, she left the bathroom and went into the living room to wait for Luke.

She didn't have to wait long. He must have showered, too for when he returned to the living room, he smelled of minty soap and that evocative woodsy cologne that stirred something deep inside her. He had changed into another pair of jeans and a navy polo shirt.

"All ready?" he asked.

"Ready," she replied.

"You look very nice," he said.

"Thank you," she returned. One of the things she liked about Luke was he was always quick to compliment her. She appreciated that, as most women would.

"Are you hungry?" he asked once they were in his truck and headed toward town.

"Actually, I am. All that fresh air and sunshine definitely stirred up my appetite," she replied.

He laughed. "It has a tendency to do that."

"It was fun today. Thank you for letting me ride one of your horses," she said.

He flashed that gorgeous smile at her. "You're a good rider. We'll plan to do it again soon."

"Thanks, I'd like that."

They rode in silence for a few minutes. It was a comfortable silence that didn't need filling with inane conversation.

It was Saturday, so hopefully tonight Peter would really cut loose and get drunk enough to confess that he'd fired the shots that had killed Big John King. She wanted that for Luke. She desperately wanted him to finally be at peace, with the killer behind bars.

However, it was a two-edge sword. While she wanted Peter to confess, she was also aware that it was possible that would be the end of any relationship with Luke.

They reached the Coyote Creek Café. Inside, the café was an homage to the area's ranchers. The walls were painted a calming green, and one wall was a painting of pastures with a herd of cattle in the distance.

They found a booth in the middle of the establishment. As they walked to the booth, several people greeted them. Carrie saw several former patients.

There was Jason Cartwell, whose wife had suffered a stroke a year before, and the Davidsons, whose little daughter had needed an emergency appendectomy, and several more who had suffered illness or injuries that had landed them either in the hospital or at the doctor's office at one time or another.

She cast a warm smile to Edward Munford, whose wife had died in the hospital three months ago from breast cancer, leaving him to raise his two-year-old son all alone. His wife, Lydia, had been pregnant when she'd been diagnosed and had refused treatment so she could deliver a healthy baby. By the time she got treatment, it had been too late. The cancer had spread throughout her entire body.

Once seated, almost immediately Stacy Wellington, one of the waitresses, appeared at their booth.

"Hi, Luke. Hi, Carrie," she greeted them with a friendly smile. Carrie had gone to school with Stacy, and she seemed to remember that Luke had dated her at one time. "What can I get for you?"

They both ordered burgers, hers with French fries and his with onion rings, and they each got a soda. Once Stacy moved away, they made small talk about the day and their plans for the next couple of days.

"If you're going back to work on Wednesday, will that interfere with our nights together at the Red Barn?" he asked.

"It shouldn't," she replied. "I might not hang out as late on the weekdays, but on the weekends, when our suspect usually gets smashed, I'll be

right there next to you as long as you need me."
She kept her voice low so nobody else nearby
might hear her.

Luke's gaze was warm on her. "I appreciate you
giving me all your free time."

She smiled at him. "Luke, you have to stop
thanking me. I'm doing this because I want to do
it."

"Okay, but I want you to think of something
I can do for you in return for everything you're
doing for me," he replied.

Just love me. The words jumped unbidden into
her head. Words she would never speak aloud to
him. For sure they were inappropriate, and she
still couldn't believe how quickly her feelings toward him had grown. "All right, I'll think about
it," she replied.

Their meals arrived, and as they ate, they got
into an animated discussion about a television
crime drama they both watched. "I'm telling you,
Powers is behind it all," she said, referencing one
of the main characters on the popular show.

"No way. It's Milton. He's the man who ordered
the hits on those two men. It's all about revenge."

Carrie laughed. "That's what they want you to
think, but I'm telling you it's Powers. Sometimes
the obvious isn't the guilty party. You just wait
and see."

"I guess we'll know by the end of the season."

She laughed again. "Or they'll leave it as a cliff-hanger and drag it into the next season."

"That's probably what they'll do," he replied.

They ate for a few more minutes. "You mentioned that one of the reasons you broke up with Rory was because he wasn't sure he wanted children. So, just how many children do you want?" he asked.

"At least two. In a perfect world, I'd have a boy and then a girl," she replied. "What about you? How many children do you want?"

"I'd like five or six," he replied.

"Five or six? How many wives do you intend to have?" she asked with a laugh.

Her laughter died on her lips as Luke glanced over her shoulder and suddenly stiffened. "There he is…the snake behind my father's murder."

Carrie glanced behind her to see Wayne Bridges with his wife and two other couples. Wayne was a tall, brown-haired man with a big barrel chest. He was a bit of a blowhard and seemed to love the sound of his own voice. As far as Carrie was concerned, he talked too loud and laughed too often, and she was glad he hadn't won the mayoral election. The group took a large corner booth, laughing and talking as they sat.

Carrie knew Wayne Bridges had run against Big John King for the mayoral position, a position that Wayne had ultimately lost to Stella Black. It was hard to believe that a man would order a hit to obtain the position of mayor in such a small town. But she knew this was what Luke believed.

Luke tapped his fingers against the tabletop, a habit she noticed he did whenever he was particularly stressed or upset. She didn't know what to believe when it came to Big John's murder. She did know that Lane, as chief of police, had admitted that it was now a cold case, with no clues or leads to move forward.

They finished their meals, left the café and headed for the Red Barn. Once again, they sat at the table close to where Peter and his buddies were seated.

"Look, it's lover boy again," Peter said once they sat down.

"I've told you before, I don't want any trouble," Luke replied.

"You were definitely looking for trouble that night when you wandered on our property," Sly Baskum said.

Carrie knew most of the men because some of her girlfriends had dated them. For the most part, she knew that the men were dirtbags misogynists and lowlifes. She also knew now that they could be brutal. They had beaten Luke badly.

"I was waiting for Peter to get out his rifle and shoot me," Luke replied.

"From what I heard, somebody else tried to

shoot you right here before," Peter replied. "Trust me, if it had been me doing the shooting, I wouldn't have missed you."

Tension filled Carrie. This was the kind of conversation Luke had been hoping for. Was it possible they were about to hear some form of a confession from the drunken ranch hand?

"Yeah, my boy here can shoot the eye out of a squirrel from a hundred yards away," Sly said and slapped Peter on the back.

"Or a man's heart?" Luke said. His words hung in the air for a long moment, until then Peter laughed uproariously.

"You think I shot your daddy?" Peter laughed again, and all the men at the table joined in. "You're barking up the wrong tree, King. But if I wanted to make that shot, it would have been a piece of cake for me."

Carrie felt Luke's tension wafting off him as the two men glared at each other. She held her breath as the stares continued. "You're some piece of work, Jeffries," Luke finally said.

"I'll drink to that," Peter said and downed his bottle of beer.

As the men at the other table returned to their own conversation, Carrie placed a hand on Luke's forearm. "Are you okay?" she asked softly.

"Yeah." He drew in a deep breath and released it slowly.

An hour later, they were back in his truck and headed back to his place. Peter and his band of creeps had left the bar fifteen minutes before.

"I thought it was going to happen tonight," he said. His voice betrayed his bitter disappointment.

"I did, too," she replied. "But I don't think Peter was really drunk enough to make a careless confession. I've seen him drunker."

"He said I was looking at the wrong person, but I still believe he did it."

"Then we continue to do what we've been doing and hope one night he gets completely smashed and accidentally confesses," she said.

"From your lips to God's ear." He turned onto the long lane that would take them to his house. "You want to come in?" he asked as he parked in front of his place.

She would have loved to spend more time with him alone, but it had been a long day, and it was late. "No, thanks. I think I'll just head on home."

He parked, and they got out and then he walked her to her car. "As always, despite what we're doing, I enjoy spending time with you," he said.

His words shot warmth straight through to her heart, and suddenly she was thinking about the kiss they had shared earlier in the day.

"I always enjoy spending time with you, too," she said. She stopped by her driver door and hoped he would kiss her again.

"Why don't I pick you up about six thirty tomorrow and we can hang out here for a while before heading back to the Red Barn?"

"Oh, Luke, there's no reason for you to drive all the way into town to pick me up when I can just meet you out here," she replied.

His features were barely discernible in the glow from his porch light. He smiled at her. "Okay, then you meet me here and we'll go from there."

"Then I guess I'll just say good night." She hesitated another long moment, hoping for a second kiss.

"Good night, Carrie," he replied and took a step back from her so she could open her door. She got into the car and released a deep sigh.

The kiss had changed everything for her. It had given her hope that he might see her as something other than a partner—that he might be seeing her as a desirable woman.

On a scale of one to ten, his kiss had been off the charts. His lips had been so soft, yet they'd had a mastery that had been thrilling. It had made her want him more than ever.

She turned onto the long, dark road that would take her back to town. Like Luke, there had been a moment tonight when she'd thought Peter was going to confess that he'd shot Big John. As he'd talked about his shooting prowess, she was certain it was going to happen. It had been a big letdown that it hadn't happened.

Maybe even drunk, Peter knew if he said anything about shooting Big John, he'd wind up in jail. Maybe he would never get drunk enough to confess to the crime. She wasn't even sure if he was really the guilty one.

She understood why he was on Luke's radar. Wayne had had a motive to want Big John out of the way, and Peter had the skill set to make that happen. But that didn't mean that either of them was good for the murder.

She was reminded of the conversation about the crime drama they both watched. Luke was convinced the obvious person was guilty, while she wasn't so sure. Peter was the obvious person, but time would tell if that made him guilty.

"Darn," she said aloud as she suddenly remembered she'd left her clothes and cosmetic bag at Luke's place. Oh well, she'd just get them tomorrow night when she was out at his place again.

She shoved all these thoughts out of her head as she saw a vehicle approaching quickly behind her. It appeared to be a truck, and it was coming on very fast. She moved over as far as she could in the lane so the driver could easily go around her.

It continued to race up directly behind her, and she gasped as the vehicle bumped into the back of her car. The steering wheel momentarily twisted out of her hands. She quickly grabbed hold of it, corrected and sped ahead.

What on earth was wrong with the driver of the truck? Was he drunk? Had he just mistakenly gotten too close to her? She stepped on the gas, wanting to get some distance from him. Before another thought could enter her mind, the truck hit her again, this time with enough force to snap her head back and then forward.

She cried out and reoriented herself just in time to see the ditch as it appeared directly in front of her. And then she slammed into it. Her body jerked around despite the seat belt, and her brain went blank.

Chapter Five

Slowly Carrie came to her senses. A hissing noise came from someplace in the front of her car. She assumed it was her radiator, but she wasn't sure. The darkness of the night fell around her, deep and profound and further disorienting her.

Her car had stopped running, and even the headlights had doused. Her seat belt had pulled agonizingly tight around her, squeezing her chest painfully. She quickly took it off, drawing several long, deep breaths in an effort to calm herself.

The airbags should have deployed, but they hadn't, and she was grateful that they hadn't. She'd always heard that airbags could hurt when they hit your face and chest.

Thankfully, she felt no real pain anywhere, so she didn't believe she was seriously hurt. She looked around for her purse, which had her phone inside, but she had no idea where her purse might be. It had been on the passenger seat before the wreck but was no longer there, and it was too dark to hunt around for it.

What she needed to do was get out of the car and get to the road so she could flag down some help. At this time of the night, on this particular road, she realized, it might be some time before another vehicle came along.

Her eyes slowly began to adjust to the dark, letting her see a little better despite the darkness. Her door was crunched, but she pushed and shoved against it with all her might and somehow managed to get it open.

She half rolled out of the car, and as she straightened up to inspect the damage, she saw the black pickup truck that had hit her parked along the side of the road. The lights were off, and the truck was idling.

Why was it just sitting there like that? Something about it seemed strangely ominous, and the air suddenly smelled not only of hot steam and oil, but also of an unknown danger.

If the driver had stopped because he'd caused the accident, then why wasn't he getting out of his truck to check on her condition? Surely that's what a normal person would do. Why was he just sitting there?

Was the driver waiting to see if he saw her and knew she was okay? Was he then going to drive off? Was it a hit-and-run and he or she just wasn't running yet?

She crouched back down and moved to the back of her car to peer around the edge of the fender. Her heart had already been beating too quickly given the wreck, but now it beat even faster.

Things just didn't feel right. For several long minutes, she remained hidden behind her car, watching and waiting to see if the truck drove away or not. She sensed something about to happen, but she couldn't anticipate what it might be. All she knew was this whole situation didn't feel right.

The driver door of the pickup suddenly flew open, and a man got out of the vehicle. In the darkness she could only see a vague silhouette, but she saw enough to be afraid. Whoever the man was, he walked with slow, heavy steps across the asphalt road, and he was carrying a rifle. Why carry a rifle to check on the victim of a car accident?

"Carrie, Carrie. Gonna shoot you deady," a deep, singsong voice said.

She froze. Wha…what was happening? Her brain tried to make sense of things, but it couldn't. He knew her name, and from his words he intended to kill her. He knew her name! Dear God, what was happening? Why was this happening? Who was this man?

She shoved a hand in her mouth to stanch the

scream that begged to be released. That voice…it was eerily familiar. But she couldn't think about that right now.

The footsteps came closer. Escape…she needed to escape. She desperately looked around for a place to hide. Would the darkness shield her if she ran away? If he did see her, a bullet from a rifle could travel a very long way far faster than she could run.

She had to do something, because he was nearly on top of her. She looked around frantically. Could she stay hidden in the deepest darkness of the ditch? Could she crawl away without him hearing her now?

She heard a faint click, and then a spear of light appeared. He had a flashlight. The words screamed through her head. *Oh God, he has a flashlight!* She now had no time to run. With the flashlight he'd find her if she hid in the ditch. He'd see her if she ran. He'd find her no matter what she did, and he apparently intended to kill her. Why? Why was this happening?

"Carrie, I'm coming for you," the deep voice said, and then he laughed. The deep burst of laughter was filled with glee.

Terror shot through her. Her chest tightened, and her throat squeezed so tight she could scarcely draw a breath. Closer…he was coming closer.

She moved as silently as possible and, not

knowing what else to do, she slid beneath the car. She lay flat, a hand once again fisted against her mouth. Quiet. She had to stay completely quiet. She watched in horror as the booted feet walked slowly around her car.

Like a child, she wanted to squeeze her eyes tightly closed and become invisible. Yet at the same time, she wanted—needed—to see where he was going and what he was doing.

Could he hear her heartbeat? It pounded so frantically in her head. Surely he could hear it, too. He was now on the driver's side of the car. The flashlight shot all around, illuminating the ditch and nearby brush.

"Carrie." Her name was a soft hiss. "Carrie, I'm going to find you, and then I'm going to kill you."

Sobs of terror blurred her vision and rose up in the back of her throat. She held them in, knowing if he heard a single sound from her, he'd find her and it would all be over.

How long before he bent down and looked beneath the car? How many minutes did she have left of her life? Sooner or later, he'd look. When he couldn't find her around the car, he'd look under it and find her.

She was now a sitting duck. How easy she'd made it for him to just point his rifle beneath the car and shoot her. Maybe she should have taken her chances running. But it was too late now.

"Carrie, I know you didn't go far. You might as well show yourself and take your medicine," the deep voice said.

Another deep sob welled up inside her, and she shoved her fisted hand more tightly against her mouth. Why was this happening? Why? Who was this man and why did he want to kill her?

She was in a nightmare, a horrible nightmare, only she couldn't wake up. She was going to die, and she would never know why.

In the distance she heard the approach of another vehicle. The flashlight clicked off, and her attacker took off running. She heard his boots back on the asphalt road and then the slam of his truck door. He took off with a squeal of tires.

At the same time, she heard the second vehicle pull to a stop. She didn't move. Fear kept her in place even as a sob finally escaped her.

"Hello? Is somebody there? Does anyone need help? Carrie, is that you?"

She recognized that deep voice. It was Luke's brother Johnny. She scooted out from beneath the car and got to her feet, sobs now ripping from her throat. "Johnny," she managed to cry. "Johnny, I'm here."

"Carrie…are you okay?" Johnny hurriedly stepped down into the ditch to meet her.

"Ye-yes…no. He was go-going to ki-kill me.

Johnny, he…he wanted to ki-kill me." The words jerked out of her amid her cries.

"Who? Carrie, what's going on? Who was going to kill you?"

"I don't kn-know. The man who w-was here before you," she replied. "Can you c-call Luke for me?" She leaned weakly against the back fender of her car.

She wanted Luke here to hold her. She needed him to wrap her in his arms and make her feel safe. Her terror still radiated through her, making it difficult for her to draw a full breath.

"The first person I need to call is Lane," Johnny replied. He pulled his phone out of his pocket and called the lawman. After telling Lane where they were on the road and that they needed a tow truck, he added that somebody had apparently tried to kill her. He hung up and then called his brother.

Carrie tried to pull herself together. Despite the heat of the night, shiver after shiver of cold chills shot through her. "Somebody should be here in just a few minutes," Johnny said. "Are you sure you aren't hurt?"

"Not physically, but I'm… I was…am…terrified."

"You're safe now." He awkwardly threw an arm around her shoulder and pulled her against his warm, strong body. "I'm not going to ask you any of the details of what happened. Lane will be here soon enough, and you can tell him everything."

She wanted to cuddle into his warmth in an effort to stanch the icy chills that continued to grip her. She needed somebody to tell her what was going on, who that man was and why he wanted to kill her.

Headlights appeared in the distance, and she tensed with a new horror. Was the man coming back? Oh God, was he coming back to kill her?

"Johnny…he's coming back," she said frantically. "He's going to kill me, and now he'll kill you, too." She gripped his arm in renewed terror.

"Nobody is going to kill you while I'm here," Johnny replied firmly. "Besides, that's Luke."

Sure enough, it was Luke's truck that pulled to a halt on the shoulder of the road. His lights illuminated the area with a welcomed brightness, and he kept them on even after he cut the engine. As he got out of the vehicle, Carrie ran toward him. She slammed into him and began to sob all over again.

He instantly wrapped his arms around her and held her tight. She buried her face in the crook of his neck as tremors shook through her body. She finally released all the deep sobs that had been trapped inside her for so long.

"Carrie, don't cry. Baby, you're okay. I've got you," he said. He rubbed his hands up and down her back in an obvious effort to comfort her.

With his arms holding her and his familiar scent

surrounding her, she felt safe for the first time since she'd careened into the ditch.

In the distance a siren wailed, letting them know Lane would be here within moments. Still, she clung to Luke as he attempted to calm her by murmuring assurances in her ear, assurances that she was safe now and he wasn't going to let anyone hurt her.

Lane pulled up, cut the screaming siren and flashing lights, and then got out of his car. "Carrie, are you okay?" he called out as he approached them.

She finally stepped out of Luke's arms. "I'm okay." She drew several deep breaths to steady herself. "A pickup truck rammed into me and I… I wound up in the ditch." Despite her best effort to stay calm and relay important information, new tears burned at her eyes as raw emotion once again surfaced.

"Then the driver…he…he got out of the truck and he had a rifle and he said he was going to kill me. And then I hid underneath the car and he had a flashlight and was looking for me. He wanted to kill me." The words tumbled out of her in a rush. "And then…then Johnny came along and the man ran back to his truck and sped away."

"Whoa, slow down," Lane replied. "Let's start at the very beginning. So, you believe this truck intentionally rammed into you to make you wreck?"

"Yes, it was absolutely intentional," she replied. "He hit me twice, and the last time I flew off the road and into the ditch." She wrapped her arms around herself as a new chill swept through her.

"Do you know the color of the pickup truck that hit you?"

"No, it was too dark to be sure, but I think it was black," she replied.

Lane looked at Johnny. "Did you see the color or recognize the vehicle?"

"No and no," he said. "The truck squealed away before I got close enough to see anything about it. I was just on my way home after playing some cards out at Sam Kaiser's place when I came upon the accident."

Lane returned his gaze to Carrie. "So, you hit the ditch, and then what happened?"

Slowly, she told him everything that had happened. As she got to the part where the man had told her he was going to kill her, Luke wrapped an arm around her shoulder and pulled her close against him once again.

"Are you sure he said your name?" Lane asked.

She nodded. "Positive. He said it several times. There was no mistaking it."

"Did you recognize the voice at all?"

She frowned thoughtfully. "I thought it sounded vaguely familiar, but I'm not so sure now. I'm not sure about anything except somebody wanted to kill me tonight." Tears once again stung her eyes and spilled onto her cheeks. She brushed them away. "I don't know who it was or why he's after me."

"Did you see anything about him?" Lane asked.

"I saw his feet. He was wearing either tan work boots or cowboy boots. That's all I saw. It was too dark to see anything else, and I was hiding under the car," she replied.

"What about height? If you saw him get out of the truck, how tall did he appear to you?"

She frowned. "I don't know…just medium height."

"What about his build? Was he heavy or thin?" Lane asked.

"I think maybe he was on the thin side," she said and then shook her head. "But I can't be sure. It was just so dark."

"Carrie, have you had problems with anyone lately? Have you fought with anybody?"

"No, nobody," she said.

"What about Dr. Holloway?" Luke said, and then he filled Lane in on her work issues.

"I can't imagine James Holloway doing something crazy like this," Lane said. "But I'll definitely check him out."

The questioning seemed to go on forever. "I'll take you home with me for the night," Luke said to her when it was all over.

"You two go ahead. I'll wait here for the tow truck," Lane said.

"I'll hang around and wait with Lane," Johnny said.

"Thank you, Johnny, for trying to make me feel better, and thank you for coming along when you did," she said. "You probably saved my life."

"No problem, Carrie," Johnny assured her.

Minutes later she was in Luke's truck and heading back to his house. "Thank you for letting me stay at your place for the night. To be honest, I was afraid to go home. I know Emily planned on being gone for the night, and I… I don't want to be all alone right now."

"I know how shook up you are, and I didn't want you to be all alone," he replied. "At least in my house you'll be safe and can get a good night's sleep."

Her cosmetic bag and the clothes she'd worn horseback riding that day were still in Luke's house. She could wear her T-shirt to sleep in, but at the moment sleep seemed far away as the horrifying events of the night kept crashing through her brain.

It didn't seem possible that it had only been earlier in the day when they had been galloping across the pasture, carefree and happy. It felt like it had been years ago that they had sat in the peaceful spot in the pasture and Luke had kissed her.

How quickly things had changed. Now her car was wrecked and somebody wanted her dead.

WHO COULD POSSIBLY be after Carrie? She was the sweetest, most giving woman Luke had ever met. It was a question that rolled over and over again in his head as he drove them back to his place.

He couldn't believe this had happened to her, that somebody had forced her car off the road with the intention of shooting her. Who could be behind such a heinous thing?

He could feel the fear that still radiated from Carrie, a fear he wished he could take away from her. He couldn't imagine the terror she must have felt when she'd been under the car and afraid of being discovered. And he couldn't imagine sending her on her way to go home alone after such a terrible scare.

Once they were inside his place, he gestured her to the sofa. She sank down and stared at the coffee table before her. He'd never seen her so pale, so utterly lost-looking. His heart positively ached for her.

"How about a drink?" he asked.

She looked up, and the depths of her beautiful eyes still held her terror. "What do you have?"

"I've got beer, whiskey and scotch—just name your pleasure." She still looked small and afraid and so vulnerable. It squeezed his heart tight to see her that way.

"Normally I'd choose a beer, but I think the night warrants something a little stronger, so I'd love a whiskey on the rocks," she replied.

"I'll be right back." He left her and went into the kitchen, where he prepared her drink and one for himself. He took off his gun belt and set it on the counter, then returned to the living room and sank down next to her.

"Thank you," she said. Her hand trembled slightly as she took the drink from him. She took a big sip, then closed her eyes as she swallowed.

"Carrie, what can I do to help?" he asked softly.

She opened her eyes and smiled, but it was a smile that didn't quite reach her eyes. "You're doing it." Her smile fell away, and she released a deep sigh. "Luke, I've never, ever been so terrified in my entire life."

"I can't even imagine." He scooted a little closer to her. He figured the best thing he could do was listen to her, as it was obvious she needed to wind down before they headed to bed. Her jeans were grass-stained, and even though she was disheveled, she still looked pretty...but frightened.

"It was like a horrible nightmare, but there was no waking up from it," she continued. "I can't imagine who the man was. He must have followed me from here. Why would somebody try to kill me, Luke?" Her gaze searched his features as if she thought he might hold the answer.

"I don't know, Carrie. I can't imagine somebody wanting to hurt you in any way. I wish I did know so Lane could get him behind bars." Luke took a drink of the whiskey, its smooth notes a pleasant warmth as it slid down his throat and into his stomach.

"Lane won't be able to make an arrest. A man driving a pickup and wearing boots describes almost every man in this town. I wasn't able to give him any kind of a description to help him find the man." Her eyes darkened with each word she spoke.

"Lane is smart. Both you and Johnny said the person squealed his tires when he drove off. Lane might be able to get a tire imprint that will let him know what kind of tire was on the vehicle, and that would definitely shorten a list of suspects."

She released a deep sigh. "I'm supposed to be helping you find your father's murderer, not worrying about my own safety," she replied and then took another sip of her drink.

"If you're still in, then we continue to go to the Red Barn in hopes that Peter will somehow confess, and at the same time we try to figure out who is after you and why. I can promise you that nobody will hurt you as long as you're with me."

"I'm still in," she replied.

"I'm glad to hear that." There was a part of him that realized he was being a jerk in even asking her about continuing to help him with his desire to catch his father's killer.

"In the meantime, what you need to think about is who might hold some kind of a grudge against you. It could be something small and insignificant to you. Also, you said you thought the voice sounded vaguely familiar. Can you try to figure out where you heard that voice before and who it belongs to?"

She released another deep sigh. "I need to think long and hard about those things, but not tonight. I just can't think any more tonight. My brain is utterly fried with everything that happened."

"Drink up, then, and we'll call it a night," he replied. He'd like to be able to tell her that everything would be better in the morning, but he couldn't say that because it wasn't true. Things would probably look just as dark for her in the light of day.

They finished their drinks. He carried the empty glasses into his kitchen and placed them in the sink. He then went back into the living room, where she had gotten up from the sofa.

Her clothes and cosmetic bag were on the table in the entryway. He grabbed them for her and then led her to the spare bedroom, hoping the whiteboards on the walls didn't bother her as she tried to fall asleep. "The sheets on the bed are clean," he said and placed the clothing and the bag on top of the light blue spread.

"Thanks, Luke…for everything." She held his gaze. In the depths of her eyes, her terror remained. Once again, she appeared achingly small and vulnerable, and his heart squeezed tight.

He reached out and drew her into his arms. She wrapped her arms around his neck and leaned her head against his chest. Desire suddenly reared up inside him, an emotion that had absolutely no place at this time—at any time. He'd pulled her close to him to comfort her, and he was a total jerk for feeling that kind of emotion right now. All he wanted to do was comfort her. He held her only for a few moments and then released her.

"If you need anything—anything at all—let me know," he said.

She nodded. "Good night, Luke," she said.

"'Night, Carrie," he said and then left the room. He went back into the kitchen and placed their glasses in the dishwasher.

He glanced up just in time to see somebody outside run past the window. He whirled around and grabbed his gun. What the hell? Nobody should be lurking around his home.

Was it possible the creep after Carrie had followed them back here? Was he now seeking a way in to kill her? With his gun tightly in his hand,

Luke quickly moved through the living room and out the front door.

Moonlight drifted down, making the landscape fairly visible. Adrenaline fired through Luke as he held his gun before him. He ran silently to the corner of the house, whirled around it and saw a figure.

"Stop or I'll shoot," he shouted.

"Don't shoot. Luke, it's me. It's Caleb."

Luke released a string of curses as he lowered his gun. "Caleb, what in the hell are you doing lurking around my house?"

"I just wanted to see Carrie and make sure she is okay. Johnny told me what happened tonight, and I was worried about her," Caleb replied. "She's my friend."

"I know she's your friend, but I could have shot you." Luke released a deep sigh. "You should have just called me if you wanted to know how she was doing."

"I'm sorry, Luke. I guess I wasn't thinking."

"It's okay, and I assure you she's okay. In fact, she just went to bed, and that's where I intend to go."

"Okay. Again, I'm sorry, and I'll just leave you alone now."

Luke watched as his brother took off toward the barn, and then he went back into the house and locked the door. The adrenaline that had rushed through him now slowly ebbed.

He headed into his own bedroom. Once there, he placed his gun on the nightstand, and then he took off his shoes and socks. He shucked his jeans and T-shirt and then got into bed wearing only his boxers.

He wasn't surprised that Caleb had been worried about Carrie. It spoke to the friendship the two of them had been building. There was no question Luke was worried about Carrie. Who had forced her off the road and then threatened to kill her?

He'd been seeing her for a couple of weeks now, and she'd never mentioned having any problems with anyone other than her boss. As far as he'd seen, she was kind to everyone. So, who was after her and why?

Was it possible it had something to do with them trying to find his father's killer? No matter how he twisted and turned it all around, he simply couldn't connect the two things.

All he could do now was make sure Carrie remained safe. From this moment on, he'd pick her up and take her home from his place. Now that he thought about it, he never should have been okay with her driving home all alone at all hours of the night in the first place.

It had been a hell of a day. First there had been

the pleasure of being back on a horse again, then the mistake of kissing Carrie.

Her lips had been so soft and filled with such heat and invitation. It hadn't felt like a mistake until it was over and he'd realized just how much he wanted to kiss her again and again. Even now the idea of kissing her once again stoked a touch of desire inside him.

Then there had been that moment when he'd thought Peter was actually going to confess to pulling the trigger and killing his father. With Peter crowing about his shooting skills, Luke had been certain he was going to crow about making the two shots that had killed Big John. But it hadn't happened.

And now this.

He turned off the lamp next to his bed and his room was plunged into darkness except for a faint ray of bright moonlight that drifted in through the window. Thoughts continued to whirl around in his head, making sleep impossible.

Had it been James Holloway who had tried to kill Carrie tonight? It had just been that morning that she'd quit her job with him. He'd obviously wanted a relationship with her. Had her quitting somehow sent him over the edge? Had he snapped and decided if he couldn't have her then nobody would? It was damned coincidental that Carrie had quit working for him that morning and then this happened.

Or was there somebody else? Somebody who was not on her radar at all? What worried him most of all was the fact that a man had tried to kill her tonight, and because he had been unsuccessful, he might try it again—the next time with success.

"Luke?" Carrie's soft voice came his doorway.

He immediately sat up. "Yeah?"

There was a moment of silence from her. "Uh… can I sleep in here with you?" The question was tentative.

He understood her need to be with somebody. Surely he could just sleep next to her with no real issues. "Come on, then," he replied.

As she went around his bed to get in on the other side, he caught a vision of her in the moonlight, her shapely legs bare beneath the T-shirt she had on. She got into bed and immediately cuddled against his side.

"Were you asleep?" she asked softly.

"No, I wasn't."

"I'm afraid to go to sleep. I'm afraid of what dreams I might have," she replied.

He threw an arm around her and allowed her to snuggle even closer to him. "I never told you that one of my secret talents is I can sniff out a nightmare from a mile away."

A small laugh escaped her. "Kind of like a drug dog?"

"Exactly like a drug dog, only I smell nightmares, and I'll wake you if I think you're having one."

"Thank you, Luke. You're the very best."

He wasn't the very best. In fact, he was the very worst. She was looking for his comfort, and he was acutely aware of each point of contact with her.

Her sleek, bare legs rubbed against his, and her full breasts were warm and soft against his side. Her breath was warm on the side of his neck, and despite all his valiant efforts to the contrary, he felt himself getting aroused.

"Luke?" She whispered his name softly.

"Yeah?"

She raised up and looked down at him, her eyes luminous in the moonlight. "Luke, I want you to kiss me. I want you to make love to me."

"Carrie, lay back down and go to sleep," he said firmly. "You're under a lot of stress right now." Her words only made the desire inside him burn hotter. But he was desperately trying to do the right thing, even though it was extremely difficult.

"I realize I'm under stress, but that has nothing to do with me wanting to make love with you. I want you, Luke. I've wanted you for some time now, and I think... I think you want me, too."

His heart suddenly beat too fast, flooding his

veins with a fiery desire he couldn't fight any longer. Her words unleashed something deep inside him, something that had been burning inside him for some time. With a groan, he reached for her and surrendered to the want he'd been fighting against for days.

Chapter Six

Luke's mouth crashed down to hers, tasting of white-hot desire and just a hint of whiskey. As he kissed her, she lay back down on the bed. She opened her mouth to him, and he took her invitation by dancing his tongue with hers.

She'd wanted this…she'd wanted him for weeks. In fact, it felt as if she'd wanted him all her life. This had little to do with what had happened this evening, although she would admit it was a perfect time to lose herself in Luke's arms.

As the kiss went on, it was as magical as it had been that afternoon. His lips were soft but commanding, and she returned the kiss with all the fever, all the intense heat he stoked in her.

His hands began to move, stroking up her back and then around to her breasts. Her nipples instantly hardened beneath her T-shirt to meet his touch.

Within minutes she was tired of the cotton material that kept him from touching her more intimately. She pulled her mouth from his and sat up. In one swift move, she pulled her T-shirt over her head and tossed it to the bottom of the bed.

"Carrie, you're so beautiful," Luke said softly.

"So are you," she replied, loving the sight of his bare chest in the faint moonlight that lit the room.

Once again, their lips met, and as he stroked her breasts, she ran her hands across his firmly muscled chest. His skin was warm and smooth, and at the same time she was enjoying touching him, she also loved him touching her.

When their kiss ended, he dragged his lips sensually along her jawline and then slowly across her collarbones. She gasped when his mouth captured one of her nipples. He teased and nipped at it, creating electric currents that raced through her entire body.

When he was finished with one, he moved to the other, giving it as much attention as he had the first. She was on fire, and he was the only one who could put it out.

Her heart cried out his name as his familiar scent surrounded her. She was utterly lost in him. All thoughts of the accident and attempted murder faded away from her mind as she embraced all things Luke.

She moved her hands lower, running down his chest and across the waistband of his boxers. It was obvious he was fully aroused, and he moaned deep in his throat with his pleasure at her touch.

She loved the sound of his moans. She loved that he was fully aroused for her, that he obviously desired her as much as she did him.

He moved one of his hands down her stomach and down to the waistband of her panties. His fingers danced there, teasing her until she was half-mindless. She held her breath, and then he was there, touching her where she most needed his touch.

More…she wanted more. As he slid her panties down, she raised her hips to allow him to draw them off her body. His hand returned to where it had been, and he began to move his fingers against her in a steady rhythm.

She raised her hips to meet his touch as a sweet tension began to build inside her. He quickened his finger movements, and she cried out his name as a sudden climax crashed over and through her.

"Luke… I want more," she whispered urgently despite the pleasure he'd just given to her. Feverishly she plucked at his boxers, wanting them off him so he could fully make love to her.

He obviously felt the same need, for he pulled his boxers down and off. He quickly moved between her legs, and she grabbed his buttocks, urging him forward.

As he eased into her, she cried out his name

once again. For a moment he remained buried deep inside her, not moving but filling her up completely. "Ah, Carrie," he whispered on a groan.

Then he began to stroke into her…slow, steady strokes that made her breathless, and a new tension quickly built up inside her. His mouth took hers again in a kiss that left them both breathless and panting.

Faster and faster he moved, taking her on a ride of pleasure she hadn't ever imagined possible. The tension built and built, higher and higher, and then she reached the peak, and as she fell over the edge, he groaned her name once again and found his own release.

Afterward they lay side by side, waiting for their breathing to return to normal. Her entire body felt warm and relaxed. She'd spent lots of time imagining what it might be like to make love to him, but her wildest fantasies couldn't compete with the reality.

It had been wonderful and magical, and she didn't want him to talk and somehow ruin it. After several minutes, she finally stirred. "I'll be right back." She slid out of the bed and grabbed her T-shirt and panties and then left the room for the bathroom in the hallway.

Now she was ready to fall asleep in his arms. feeling safe and secure and loved—if only for a night. Once she was cleaned up and redressed, she went back to his bedroom.

She smelled the scent of minty soap and knew he had gotten up and cleaned up. He'd pulled his boxers back on. "Luke, please don't say anything," she said as she got back into the bed. "We can talk about all this in the morning if you really feel the need. I just want to go to sleep now." She moved close to his side. "Deal?"

He hesitated a long moment. "Deal," he finally said.

He wrapped an arm around her, and she snuggled into him. Within minutes she was sound asleep.

She awakened the next morning with bright sunshine streaming through the window. Luke was no longer in bed with her, but his pillow still held the imprint of his head.

She remained in the bed, thinking about the night before and what she and Luke had shared. He'd been a wonderful, generous lover, and she wanted him all over again. But now it was time to get out of bed and face the new day.

She was surprised that when she moved to get up, her body protested. She ached all over, and it wasn't from Luke's lovemaking. She assumed it was from the car accident. She must have been banged around more than she realized.

The accident…she needed to call her insurance

company and arrange for a rental car. It would be nice if Lane contacted her this morning to tell her that he'd arrested the man who had caused the accident—the man who had wanted to kill her. Unfortunately, she knew that probably wasn't going to happen.

Despite the warmth of the bed, in spite of what she and Luke had shared the night before, a chill walked up her spine as she thought of the accident. Of course, it hadn't been an accident at all. It had been on purpose, with the sole desire to kill her.

Who? Who would want to kill her? And why? She thought again of the man's voice. She still had the feeling she'd heard it before, but where? She just couldn't make a connection right now.

With these disturbing thoughts rolling around in her head, she finally pulled herself up. When she went into the hallway on her way to the spare bedroom, the air smelled of freshly brewed coffee.

Once in the bedroom, she pulled on the jeans and blouse she'd worn to go horseback riding the day before and then went back to the guest bathroom to brush her hair and freshen up. Thank goodness she'd left her cosmetic bag here so she could now put on a touch of makeup.

When that was done, she headed into the kitchen, where she found Luke seated at the table with a cup of coffee before him. "Good morning," she said.

"Good morning to you," he replied and immediately got out of his chair. "Sit and I'll pour you a cup of coffee."

"Thank you," she replied and eased down into a chair.

"How did you sleep?" he asked.

"Good, except this morning I'm definitely feeling all kinds of aches and pains from the car crash."

He turned and looked at her in alarm. "Do you need to see a doctor?" His voice held a wealth of concern.

"No, nothing like that," she quickly replied. "I'm just sore in places I didn't know I had."

"I'm sorry to hear that." He placed a cup of coffee before her and then sank back down across from her. He eyed her with concern. "Are you sure you don't need to see a doctor?"

"I'm sure," she assured him. "I'll be just fine."

"God, Carrie, you could have been killed from the car wreck alone."

"I know, but I wasn't. I'm here and I'm alive, and I'm very grateful for that."

He smiled. "That makes two of us. Now, how about I make us some breakfast?" he said.

"I don't want you to wait on me, Luke. You've done more than enough for me already." Memories of the night before suddenly filled her head once again, reminding her of how much pleasure she'd found in his arms. "Really, all I need from you now is a ride home."

"Before I take you home, I'm making myself some breakfast, and it's no big deal to add an extra egg or two and some toast for you." He grinned at her. "It's one of my secret talents—I make really good scrambled eggs with cheese and some cut-up ham and a little red and green pepper. Surely you don't want to leave here without tasting them."

She returned his smile. "Okay, you talked me into it. Now I have to try your scrambled eggs, especially since making them is one of your secret talents."

"You got it." Once again, he got up from the table and went to the cabinet, where he took out a skillet, and then he began pulling ingredients out of the refrigerator.

"Do you cook often?" she asked.

"Before my dad's death, I almost always made and ate my own meals here. Since then, I often eat at the big house with Mom and my siblings."

"Are you a good cook?" she asked, hoping to head him off from any grief or anger that might fill him concerning his father's murder. She also didn't want to give him a chance to talk about what had happened between them the night before. He'd told her he regretted kissing her. She feared he'd tell her he definitely regretted making love to her.

"I like to think I am," he replied. "What about you? Can you cook?"

"I don't do it often, but yes, I can cook. After my mom died, I had to learn pretty quickly. My dad didn't know how to cook, so if we wanted to eat, I realized I'd need to do the cooking."

For the next few minutes, they talked about what kinds of food they enjoyed cooking and various recipes. "I have to say, I'm vaguely surprised by your culinary skills," she said as he poured the egg mixture into the skillet.

"Why?"

"I've always thought of you as this big, macho guy who didn't cook or clean," she replied. "I figured you probably had a small group of women who happily did those things for you."

He laughed. "That's really what you thought?"

"Definitely women lining up to help take care of you," she replied. "You have a reputation as a ladies' man."

He placed four slices of bread in the toaster and punched down the buttons and then returned to stir the eggs. "Before Dad's murder, I was dating to find my significant other. I would date somebody a couple of times, and when I realized she wasn't the one for me, I'd move on to date somebody else. I don't know how else to find the perfect mate other than doing that."

"I get where you're coming from," she said. "A man can do that, but if a woman dates a lot and too often, she's sometimes called rather nasty names."

"Yeah, and that's unfortunate. But I realize I got a reputation as a heartbreaker, even though I never, ever intended to hurt anyone that I dated." He removed the eggs from the burner at the same time the toast popped up.

At least she was happy that they were talking about things other than what they'd shared the night before. She didn't want to hear him talk about how wrong it had been or that it had been a complete mistake, like he had when they'd only shared that simple kiss.

They had just finished eating when a knock sounded on the door. Luke answered. It was Lane, and he had Carrie's purse in his hand. "I thought you might need this," he said as he gave it to her. "We recovered it from your car."

"Thank you," she said as she took it from him. She checked inside, glad to see her phone and her wallet. "Thank goodness. Now once I charge my phone, I need to make some phone calls to see about getting a rental car."

"Your insurance will probably declare your car totaled," Lane said. "It suffered pretty severe front and back damage. You were lucky to get out of it without any injuries. And speaking of injuries, needless to say I have nobody under arrest yet concerning the events of last night."

"I didn't think you would," she replied. Once

again, a cold chill waltzed up her back. Who was the man been who wanted her dead?

"We towed your car to Myers's lot," Lane continued. Ty Myers owned the only car dealership and garage in town. "He's waiting to hear from you, and he'll be able to give you the rest of your belongings that were in the car."

"I'll call him as soon as I get home and charge my phone," she replied.

Lane raked a hand through his thinning brown hair, a frown creasing his wide forehead. "Carrie, until we find the person who attacked you last night, it's important that you keep yourself as safe as possible. I don't have the manpower to put a security detail on you. You have to pay attention to your surroundings when you're out and about and make sure you aren't putting yourself at risk. Try to make sure you aren't alone whenever possible when you do have to go out."

Each word he said only made the chill inside her grow colder. "Carrie, if that man's intent was to kill you, it's quite possible he'll try again."

Even though logically she knew these things, hearing them spoken out loud only made it all worse. The same questions whirled around in her head with an awful dread. Who wanted her dead? And why?

ONCE LANE LEFT, they cleaned up the kitchen and then got into Luke's truck so he could take her home. He made sure to have his gun and holster riding his hip. Nobody was going to take him by surprise, especially when Carrie was with him.

Throughout the morning he'd tried to find the perfect time to talk to her about their lovemaking the night before. But the moment hadn't presented itself. However, it was a conversation he intended to have with her before they said goodbye for the day.

Jeez, they hadn't even used birth control. Things had flared out of control between them so fast he hadn't even thought about a condom. Bad on him. But it was important she understand that it was a fluke and didn't change the way he viewed her. She was a friend, and that was all she'd ever be.

"I'm so glad to have my purse and phone back," she said as he pulled away from the King ranch. "I was dreading having to replace everything."

"Yeah, it's good you have it back. Replacing everything like your driver's license and credit cards would have been a real pain."

"So, what time are we planning to go to the Red Barn tonight?" she asked.

He shot her a look of surprise. "Are you sure you're really up for that tonight?"

"I'm not stopping my life because of what's happened," she replied firmly. "What am I supposed to do, cower in my house until Lane arrests somebody? Lord knows when that's going to happen."

"It's your call, Carrie. I'll tell you what—why don't I pick you up about four and I'll cook dinner for you? We can just hang out around the ranch and skip the Red Barn for tonight."

He suddenly thought about that night when they stepped out of the Red Barn and somebody had shot at them. Was it possible the shooter had made an attempt on Carrie's life that night? Had she been the shooter's target?

A new tension tightened his chest at the thought. He needed to mention it to Lane. Maybe Luke needed to keep Carrie as close to him as possible to make sure she stayed safe. Right now, he couldn't imagine what his life would be like without her in it. She'd not only been his partner, but she was also his very sanity amid the sea of rage and grief that still rocked through him.

"That sounds perfect," she replied and cast him one of her warm, beautiful smiles. "But tomorrow night we're back on Peter watch at the Red Barn."

He pulled up in front of her house. "Just sit tight. I'll walk you to your door," he said. He cut his engine, got out and hurried around to the passenger door.

As he did, he looked first to the left and then to the right, making sure there was nobody lurking in the area either on foot or in a car. Satisfied there was no danger to her, he opened the passenger door, and she got out.

"Remember what Lane told you," he said as he walked her to her front door. "Stay aware of everyone around you, and keep trying to remember where you heard that man's voice before. Keep your door locked—don't open it for just anyone, and I'll see you back here around four."

She unlocked her door and then turned back to him. "Thank you for everything, Luke. I don't know what I would have done without you last night."

Minutes later he was back in his truck and heading home. He'd find a time later to talk to Carrie about what had happened between them the night before. She was a chill woman and would understand that things had just gotten out of control and that it wouldn't—it *shouldn't*—ever happen again.

Dammit, he didn't want a girlfriend. He didn't have time to woo anyone. He didn't have time for romance. He just wanted to catch his father's killer. When he'd come up with the idea of catching Peter bragging about his gun skills and confessing that he'd made the two shots on Big John, he'd never dreamed it would take this long.

Maybe he was wrong about Peter being the shooter. He knew the ranch hand had no personal animosity toward Big John. Despite him being a drunk and disgusting, Luke assumed he didn't have much of a criminal record or Lane would be looking at him closely. But at the time of the murder, Peter's boss, Wayne Bridges, had had a major reason to want Big John dead. And Luke believed Peter's skills with a rifle could be bought.

No, he wasn't wrong...unless... He shoved thoughts of his brother away. He didn't want to believe that Caleb was capable of killing his own father.

And just who in the hell was after Carrie?

All these thoughts whirred around inside his head even after he got home. Once there he took two steaks out of the freezer for dinner that night and then headed outside.

He was on the way to the stables when he ran into his brother Johnny. For the past couple of weeks, Luke had been trying to avoid his older sibling whenever possible.

"Hey, Luke," Johnny said as the two got closer to each other. "Where are you headed?"

"I thought I'd ride a few fences and check for breaks," Luke replied.

"Ribs feeling okay now?"

"Finally, they're much better," Luke replied.

"It was a hell of a mess last night."

"Yeah, thanks for being there for Carrie. She told me you were very nice to her before anyone else arrived," Luke replied.

"It was no problem. You're spending a lot of time with her."

"Yeah, I like her."

"Have you given any thought to the horse-breeding information I'd like you to find?"

The question poked at the anger that was never far from the surface. "I've been a little busy, Johnny. I don't know if you care anymore, but somebody murdered our father."

Johnny's eyes flashed darkly, and he took an aggressive step toward Luke. "You need to stop saying that, Luke. Dammit, of course I care about Dad, but I can't do anything about it. Lane is continuing to investigate and I've gotten on with living my life, something we all should be doing now."

Johnny drew a deep breath. "Luke, I need you here at the ranch. I need you to be present both physically and mentally. I just had to hire another ranch hand because you've been so absent around here. And if you're still doing crazy things to find Dad's murderer, keep in mind that it hasn't been that long since you were half beaten to death."

"I'm not doing crazy things, and my biggest worry right now is about Carrie. Somebody tried to kill her last night, and I intend to keep her as close to me as much as possible."

It was Luke's turn to take a deep breath. "I'm sorry you had to hire another man to help out around here, but maybe that's for the best, because I have a lot on my plate right now."

Johnny held his gaze for a long moment. "You know I love you, Luke, and I don't like to see you still struggling with your anger over the murder. You need to let it go and move on with your life."

"I'm trying to do that," Luke replied with a touch of a new anger rising up inside him. "Just because I'm not doing it your way doesn't mean I'm not doing it the right way for me."

"Don't be angry with me for caring about you," Johnny retorted. "I want to heal my family. Dad would hate the way we've all pulled apart instead of all coming together."

"I'll be healed when Dad's killer is behind bars. I'll be good once the creep who tried to kill Carrie last night is in jail," Luke replied.

"You need to leave both of those things to Lane," Johnny said.

"Yeah, right." Luke released a small laugh. "He has no clue who's responsible for either crime. He doesn't even have any suspects in mind."

"Luke, I just want you to get back to enjoying life. You can't mourn forever. Dad wouldn't have wanted that for you. He wouldn't like to see you the way you've been."

"I know, and I am enjoying spending time with Carrie. Of course, now I'm worried sick about her safety."

It was true. If anything happened to Carrie, he feared he'd drown in his own grief. She was the only bright spot in his life right now, even though he wasn't romantically involved with her.

Johnny reached out and patted Luke on the shoulder. "Let me know if I can do anything to help you, Luke. I know we've been at odds lately, but I'm here for you if you need me."

"Thanks, Johnny, I appreciate that," Luke replied. "And now I better get going. I'm picking up Carrie about four today and bringing her back here to hang out."

Minutes later Luke was on Storm's back and riding along the edge of the huge pastureland. His thoughts were still on his brother. There were only sixteen months between him and Johnny, and the two had always been close—and competitive with each other.

Growing up, if Johnny did something, then Luke worked to do it, too. They both had vied for attention from their parents, with Johnny often winning that battle.

Luke loved his brother, but he was frustrated that Johnny didn't share Luke's rage, his driving need to find out who killed their father. Johnny seemed content now to work the ranch and share his life with Chelsea. Luke didn't understand how Johnny—how *anyone*—had just moved on from the murder.

He didn't know how his sister was dealing with things. Since Ashley had moved back to town and was working in her shop, he hadn't seen much of her.

He rode for almost two hours, checking the

fence line and on the huge herd of cattle that called the pasture home. He then headed back to his place for a hot shower and to get ready to pick up Carrie.

At four o'clock he pulled up in her driveway. She must have been looking out for him, as she immediately came out of the front door and ran to the passenger side of his truck. She was clad in a pair of black jeans and a bright yellow blouse, and the smile she wore was like a ray of sunshine.

"Hi," she said once she was settled in the seat next to him.

"Hi. Don't ever do that again," he said with reproach.

Her bright smile instantly doused. "Do what?"

"You ran out your door without even looking around outside. A bad guy could have been waiting in the bushes next to your porch and grabbed you before I could even get out of my truck. You should have waited for me to come up to the door to get you," he said.

"Oh... I... I guess I wasn't thinking. I saw your truck and..." Her voice trailed off.

"I don't mean to scold you, but Carrie, you have to be on your toes all the time. I will walk you to and from my truck as long as this man in on the loose. Again, I'm sorry for coming down hard on you."

"No, you're right," she instantly agreed. "And I won't make the same mistake twice."

"Good." He flashed her a grin. "Now, how was your day?" he asked as he backed out of the driveway.

"Busy," she replied. "Emily called me several times when my phone was dead, so as soon as my phone was charged, I called her back."

"Did you tell her what happened to you?"

"I did, and she was horrified. We agreed that when our work hours are the same, we'll ride together."

"Good, that's smart," he agreed.

"After talking to Emily, I made the accident report with my insurance company, and I have a rental car set up for me to get tomorrow. I also had to call Dr. Morris to let him know I couldn't start for him Wednesday but instead could start Thursday. What about you? How was your day?"

"It was okay. I did a little riding and then had a minifight with Johnny," he said.

"A minifight about what?"

He told her about the conversation he'd had with his brother. "I guess I just find it frustrating that he doesn't feel the same way I do."

"You know he's only trying to look out for you," she said.

"Yeah, I know. He just doesn't understand the drive I have to solve Dad's murder. Speaking of murder, did you hear any more from Lane today?"

"No, nothing, but I honestly didn't expect to. I

spent the day trying to think of anyone who might have an issue with me. I also tried to remember where I'd heard that voice before, but I had no luck on either count."

"Hopefully it will come to you very soon. You remembering where you heard that voice might be the only way to catch this guy."

"I know—don't remind me. So, I'm looking forward to a home-cooked dinner from you tonight," she said.

He grinned at her again. "I hope you're satisfied at the end of it."

"I'm not real critical when it comes to food. I just like to eat."

They talked about food until they arrived at his place. Once inside, he took off his gun and set it on the counter, then he offered her a seat at the table while he got busy on the evening meal.

Before he'd left to pick her up, he'd put two big potatoes in the oven to bake and had made a salad. All he had left to do was cook the steaks, dress the salad and warm up some garlic bread.

He'd also called Lane and told him he thought the gunfire at the Red Barn might have been the first attempt on Carrie's life—something he wasn't going to talk about with Carrie unless she brought it up. She had enough on her plate to worry about without that additional concern.

He worked while they talked, and before long

the meal was ready and on the table. "Oh my gosh, Luke, this is the best steak I've ever tasted," she said after taking a couple of bites.

"Thanks. It's all in the secret seasoning I use."

"Are you going to tell me what it is?"

He grinned at her. "I'll have to think about it," he said teasingly.

He wanted to keep things light with her this evening. She'd been through a terrible trauma the night before, and he wanted to be her soft place to fall, like she had been for him in the past.

Even though he still needed to make her understand that just because they had made love the night before, it didn't mean they were romantically involved or lovers in the true sense of the word. But tonight wasn't a good time to bring it up.

Tonight, she just needed to relax and chill out, so as they ate, he entertained her with funny stories from his childhood. He loved to hear her laughter, and he made sure to make her laugh over and over again.

He told her about funny fights with his siblings. There had been a time when they were all angry with their mom, and so they had decided to run away from home.

They'd only run as far as the backyard area. They had dragged lumber from the barn to the yard and built a sort of shelter with the old wood and bedsheets.

"We were determined we were going to live out there forever. We each had taken something from the kitchen before we left. We had one apple, a cupcake, a bag of pretzels and I can't remember what else, but I can tell you splitting an apple four ways doesn't give anyone much apple," he said.

She laughed. "Why were you all so mad at your mother?"

"I don't even remember now," he admitted.

"So, how long were you out there?" she asked.

"Until darkness started to fall and the night insects started to sing. Ashley was the first one to go in. She was sure something was going to eat us all. Caleb was quick on her heels. He was positive something was going to kill us. Johnny and I managed to wait it out until about ten or so. We were both sleepy and just wanted the comfort of our own beds. The next day we had to clean up the mess we'd made in the yard, and we didn't try to run away again."

"So, you all learned an important lesson," she replied.

"Yeah, we learned that our beds were softer than the ground and a home-cooked meal was better than an apple split four ways," he replied, making her laugh once again.

They finished eating, and together they cleaned up the dishes. "Now that I ate so much, I'm ready for a walk," she said.

"That sounds good to me." He pulled his gun belt back on, and as he did, her eyes darkened.

"I wish you didn't have to wear that," she said softly.

"Carrie, I'm going to wear it until Lane finds the man who's after you. I told you before, I will keep you safe as long as you're with me."

"Thanks, Luke. I can't tell you how much I appreciate you."

Her words warmed his heart. They stepped outside and he threw an arm over her shoulder as they began a leisurely walk toward the barn. As always, the scent of her eddied in his head, a slightly exotic scent that continually stirred him on a primal level.

"It's another nice evening," she said.

"It won't be too long before it's going to get miserably hot," he replied.

"Maybe it will be a mild summer."

"That would be nice," he said.

As they got closer to the barn, he saw Caleb standing outside with Leroy Hicks. Luke's chest tightened. Leroy had worked for the Kings, but right before Big John's death, he had fired Leroy for theft and being drunk on the job.

At the time Leroy had made all kinds of horrible threats against Big John and the King ranch, but he'd had an alibi for the time of the murder, which had been corroborated by several other people.

Even though Leroy hadn't killed Big John, Luke

couldn't believe his younger brother was now friends with the weasel. Luke couldn't be sure, but he believed the two of them were into something they shouldn't be in, but hell if Luke knew what it was.

It was only a month ago that Caleb and Leroy had been hanging out by the barn when several men on horseback began shooting at them. Johnny and Luke had gone after the men but had been unable to see who they were or find out why they had been attacking Caleb and Leroy.

Caleb had insisted he had no idea why the men had been shooting at them, but Luke and Johnny weren't sure they believed Caleb. Something was going on with Caleb, but damned if Luke could figure it out.

One thing was for sure—Luke believed Leroy was a bad influence on his brother, but there was nothing he could do about it. He couldn't exactly demand his adult brother pick his friends better.

As they met the two, Luke introduced Carrie to Leroy.

"Nice to meet you," Carrie replied and then smiled at Caleb. "How are you doing, Caleb? Are you still working on paintings for your show?"

"Definitely." He looked at her intently. "How are you? Johnny told me what happened last night."

"I'm doing fine, thanks to your brother." She smiled at Luke.

"You want to come in and see a couple of my paintings?" Caleb asked Carrie, totally surprising Luke.

"You know I'd love to," she replied. "I've been interested in your painting for a while now."

"Leroy, you wait out here with Luke. Carrie, come on in and I'll show you a few of them."

As Carrie followed Caleb into the barn, a new tension tightened Luke's chest. Was it possible Caleb would tell Carrie something about the day of their father's murder? It was possible that in the next few minutes Carrie might hear something that would either damn his brother or exonerate him.

Chapter Seven

Carrie followed Caleb through the barn and into the doorway of his apartment, a small room with a single bed and a chest of drawers. There was a doorway that she assumed went into a bathroom and a curtain, behind which she assumed he hung his clothes. The whole area smelled of booze, weed, oil paint and turpentine.

An easel in the corner held a large blank canvas. "Looks like you're getting ready to start on a new one," she said.

"Yeah, I finished my last one three days ago."

"How long does it generally take you from start to finish on a painting?" she asked. She was aware that this was a huge moment, and she had no idea what to expect. Luke had told her Caleb spent a lot of time in the woods taking pictures of flowers and that he'd never shown his paintings to anyone except Leroy.

She had to be careful what she said and how she

acted in order for Caleb to be completely comfortable with her. She knew what information Luke wanted her to get out of him and she'd do her best, but she couldn't push it.

"Usually, it takes me three to four days per painting, but then it takes several days for me to fill my creative well again," he replied. He gestured her toward the bed. "Have a seat."

"Thanks." She sat gingerly on the edge of the bed. The sheet that covered the mattress appeared dingy and gray. There was no top sheet or bedspread.

"My painting has always been my therapy. My dad didn't understand me, and he didn't like me very much. He thought I was useless because I didn't want to work on the ranch like Johnny and Luke. He didn't understand the dreams I had for myself."

"Oh, Caleb, I'm sure your father loved you very much."

He cast her a crooked smile. "Yeah, well, I'm pretty sure he didn't. Anyway, this is one of the paintings I intend to be in my show." He went behind the curtain and returned with a small painting of a single flower. Dewdrops glistened on the reddish-pink petals, and each leaf was painted in exquisite detail.

"Oh, Caleb, it's stunning," she exclaimed. "I never dreamed you were so talented."

"Thanks, Carrie." He smiled at her, obviously pleased.

"This is part of a collection just titled Nature. It's a group of painting that are mostly flowers. Then I have another collection entitled Feelings."

"Could I see something from that collection?" she asked. She was genuinely impressed by his work.

"Uh…okay." He disappeared behind the curtain once again, and when he reappeared he had two larger paintings in his hands. Carrie caught her breath, hoping he didn't see her complete shock.

She'd been expecting more greenery and flowers, but these paintings were abstracts in bold black and reds. The strokes were strong and more like slashes. The paintings portrayed violence and anger, and she found them deeply disturbing.

"So, what do you think?" Caleb's pale blue eyes held her gaze intently.

"I think it's obvious they are filled with a lot of emotion," she replied slowly. "I see a lot of sadness and unresolved issues."

"Exactly," Caleb said, once again obviously pleased by her words. "I'm glad you get that, Carrie. It's exactly what I was going for." He smiled at her. "I knew in my gut that you'd understand them…that you'd understand me."

"Do you want me to see more of your work?"

Caleb frowned. "No, I think this is enough for

today." He placed the paintings back behind the curtain as Carrie stood from the bed. "I'm so glad that you *get* me," he said as he opened the door for them to walk out.

"When are you planning your show?" she asked.

"I'm now thinking about having it during the big Fourth of July celebration in town."

On the Fourth of July, the town went all out, with a fair during the day where vendors sold their fares. There was a contest for the best apple pie and another one for eating hot dogs. It was a day of fun, and then at night there was a carnival and a huge firework display. The new mayor, Stella Black, had promised that this year would be even better than ever.

"That would be a perfect opportunity for you," she said.

"Just remember that what you saw and what I said is our business and doesn't need to be shared with anyone."

"I won't forget that, Caleb," she replied.

They stepped back out into the sunshine, where Luke and Leroy were waiting. "You should feel very honored, Carrie," Leroy said. "Caleb hasn't shown his paintings to anyone but me."

"I do feel very honored," she replied and offered a warm smile to Caleb.

"You're almost family," Caleb replied. "And I

feel like I can trust you. You're a kindred soul, Carrie."

"Come on, kindred soul," Luke said. "We need to finish our walk before nightfall."

"We'll see you two later," she said, and then she and Luke continued walking in the direction of the big house.

"So, what did you see?" Luke asked as soon as they were out of earshot of Caleb and Leroy.

"First of all, he told me that your father never understood him and didn't love him," Carrie said.

"I think that's been his excuse for all his bad behavior over the years. Dad didn't love him, so now he's a drunk and a drug user. Dad didn't love him, so he never had to take responsibility for any of his actions. It's been a big song and dance from him since he was a teenager."

"I don't think it's a song and dance. I think that's what he truly believes. The first painting he showed me was of a flower. It was absolutely beautiful. He has real talent, Luke."

"You think?" he asked in surprise.

"Well, I'm not exactly an art critic, but that flower was completely, breathtakingly gorgeous." She paused a moment and then continued, "And now do you want to hear the bad news?"

He frowned. "There's bad news?"

She nodded. "He then showed me two paintings that were definitely disturbing."

"Disturbing how?" Luke asked, slowing his footsteps as they talked.

"They were all black and red strokes. They looked like they were filled with rage and darkness. Looking at them, I really think your brother maybe needs help from a real therapist. Have you ever tried to get him help?"

"Several times. I know my mother has encouraged him to get some help, but he refuses. He keeps telling us his art is his therapy. So, what do you think about the idea of him being the one who killed my father?"

She could feel the sudden tension that wafted from him, and she wished she could take it away but knew she couldn't. "I don't know, Luke. After seeing the rage in those paintings, I wouldn't exclude him from the possibility."

He sighed. "That's what I was afraid you would say. Dammit, why has this been so difficult? This is a small town, and not many people could have taken the shots that killed my father."

His anger quickly rose to the surface. "And why in the hell can't Lane find one sick twist who wants to attack you?"

"Luke…" She grabbed his hand and squeezed it. "Remember that anger creates stress, and stress isn't good for you."

"Carrie, tell me the truth. Aren't you angry that somebody is after you? Aren't you angry that somebody tried to kill you last night?" He stopped in his tracks and gazed at her searchingly.

"No, that doesn't make me angry. It makes me completely stressed."

He stared at her for a long moment and then laughed. "Woman, you are something else," he exclaimed.

His anger seemed to completely disappear as they walked on. In fact, he was far less angry now than he had been when they'd first started their quest. His bursts of anger came less and less frequently and were shorter in length.

She was encouraged that he hadn't brought up their lovemaking. She was elated that he hadn't tried to diminish it or take it back.

They walked to the big house and then turned around to walk back. "Why don't we sit on your dock and listen to the fish jump?" she suggested.

"We can do that," he agreed.

A few minutes later, they were side by side on the wooden structure that extended out into the water. Trees surrounded them, and for the first time since her crash the night before, she truly relaxed.

"Sometimes you have to push all the bad stuff out of your mind for a while and just enjoy being," she said. "I have a feeling you don't allow yourself to do that very often."

"When I'm with you, it's easier to do, but when

I'm all alone, the bad stuff always seems to win out," he admitted.

"You need to work on that."

He grinned at her. "Yes, ma'am."

They remained seated on the dock talking about all kinds of things until darkness fell. They talked about their politics—they were both independents. They discussed favorite music. He was country-western, and she enjoyed more pop. However, they both liked oldies. Each and every subject they talked about make her feel like she knew him better and he knew her more.

"I should probably get you home," he said once darkness began to fall. They rose from the dock.

"Yeah, the next couple of days are going to be busy for me before I start work again on Thursday morning."

"Do you need a ride to Myers's tomorrow to pick up the rental car?" he asked once they were in his truck and headed back toward town.

"No. Emily has the day off and is taking me to get it, but thanks for asking."

"Carrie, remember that you need to watch where you go and who you allow to get close to you," he said. "You need to be aware of your surroundings at all times."

She couldn't help the way her chest tightened. "I know." Just that quickly she was back under her car, holding her breath and waiting for a killer to bend down and find her. She couldn't breathe as chills raced up and down her spine.

Don't let him find me. Oh God, please, please don't let him bend down and find me. The words rolled around and around in her head. She was trapped in the memories in her mind.

She stared out the side window, drawing deep breaths in an effort to calm herself down. She reminded herself that she wasn't beneath the car anymore. She'd survived both the car accident and the man attempting to kill her. He hadn't found her and she was safe…safe here with Luke.

She couldn't do anything about what had already happened, but she could think about where she'd heard that man's voice before. Identifying the voice might be the only way he'd be caught.

"Are you okay?" Luke's voice sliced through her troubling thoughts.

"I'm fine. I was just reminding myself how important it is that I try to identify the voice of the man who wants me dead," she replied.

"It's probably one of those things that the harder you try to remember, the harder it will be to remember," he said.

"I have a feeling remembering is the only way to catch this man. He certainly didn't leave any clues behind."

As they pulled up in front of her house, she was grateful that Emily had turned the porch light on for her. "Sit tight," he said as he parked in the driveway.

She watched as he walked around the front of the truck to her door. As he opened it, he had one hand on the door handle and his other hand on the butt of his gun. He looked big and strong and made her feel incredibly safe.

As they walked to her door, she found herself following his gaze from the left to the right, seeking any danger that might exist in the dark shadows of the night.

When they reached the door, she stood with her back against it, and he stood in front of her. "Thanks, Luke, for taking my mind off things for a little while. It was nice to just chill out for a bit and not think about anything too important."

"Back at you," he replied softly. "Carrie, if you ever feel unsafe or that you're in a dangerous situation, day or night, I'm just a phone call away. Even if for some reason you're just afraid, call me."

"I appreciate that." He stood close to her— intimately close.

Her breath caught in her chest at his nearness, and she raised her face to him, hoping that he would take her in his arms, hold her tight and kiss her. Oh, she wanted him to kiss her once again.

She parted her lips in anticipation as he leaned toward her, his eyes darkening with something delicious. At the last moment, he jerked back from her.

"Good night, Carrie." His voice was deeper than usual.

"Good night, Luke," she replied. "Are we still on for the Red Barn tomorrow night?"

"That's up to you. Why don't I call you tomorrow afternoon and we can talk about it?"

"Okay, then I'll talk to you tomorrow."

Once inside her house, she leaned with her back against the door and thought about that moment when she'd been sure he was going to kiss her. But he hadn't.

This had started out as a desire on her part to get to know the man she'd had a crush on better, but it had grown into something much more, something much deeper.

She felt as if she knew Luke better than she'd ever known a man in her life. He had been vulnerable to her with his innermost feelings, and she had been vulnerable to him in the same way.

She loved spending time with him. He made her laugh, and he made her think. He challenged her in good ways, and each touch from him warmed her in a way no other man's touch had ever done before.

She was in love with him.

The realization slammed into her with a huge joy and more than a little fear. More importantly, she believed Luke was falling in love with her, too.

However, she couldn't see how this all would

end. When he tired of going to the Red Barn on the off chance he'd catch Peter confessing to shooting his father, would he then just kick her to the curb? Would he be in a head space to embrace any love he might feel for her, or would he allow his anger and his need for revenge to keep him isolated and all alone?

With a sigh, she pushed herself off the door and headed upstairs. Another thought jumped into her head, bringing with it a chill of fear. She would never know how her relationship with Luke wound up if she was murdered.

FOR THE FIRST time since his beatdown, Luke put in a full day of work doing chores around the ranch. It felt good being out in the sunshine and working again. He not only did chores, but he also rode with Johnny for about an hour to inspect the herd.

He'd forgotten how much he loved all things ranching, like his father had before him and his brother did now. He loved the smell of the pastures and working with the herd of cattle that provided their livelihood.

He and Johnny made good partners. They were almost always on the same page when it came to the business. His brother had mentioned the horse-breeding program again that day, and Luke had told him he'd get to it in time. Thankfully, Johnny had dropped the subject.

Luke finally stopped for a break at around two and called Carrie.

"Did you get your rental car all squared away?" he asked when she answered.

"I did. At least I have wheels now to start at Dr. Morris's office ," she replied.

"What do you think about going to the Red Barn tonight?"

"You know me, Luke. I'm in—just tell me what time to be ready."

He thought about picking her up early so they could just hang out and talk before going to the bar, but then he changed his mind. "Why don't I pick you up around eight? I promise I won't keep you out too late since you're getting ready to start your new job ."

She laughed, that musical sound that he never got tired of hearing. "I appreciate that, but I'm a big girl. I can stay out as late as you need me and still be on my toes for work."

"Okay, then I'll see you tonight at eight."

He frowned as he hung up. He was getting too close to Carrie. He was starting to miss her when they were apart. He hated when he had to tell her goodbye, which he'd never expected. He thought about her first thing in the morning, and she was on his mind when he fell asleep at night.

He'd almost kissed her the night before. It had taken all his willpower not to kiss her again. He told himself he didn't need or want her as a lover, and yet he couldn't forget how soft and warm and giving she'd been in bed.

She had been an incredible lover, and if he had his way, he'd take her to bed over and over again. He'd explore more depths of the passion he felt for her. But that would be an enormous mistake. He already feared he'd sent her some mixed signals.

Somehow, he had to keep his emotional distance from her from now on. He'd already shared too much of himself with her. He wanted to keep her as his partner in crime, but it was time he maintained a healthy distance from her emotionally so his signals weren't mixed and she definitely understood they were just partners and nothing more.

At four o'clock he knocked off work and went in to take a shower. When he was cleaned up, he decided to go to the big house to eat dinner. He hadn't seen his mother for several days and hadn't eaten with her for far too long.

As he walked toward his childhood home, Johnny and Chelsea joined him. "It's nice to see you coming to dinner," Chelsea said. "I know your mother has missed seeing you there lately."

"Yeah, I've missed seeing her, too." To be honest, it had been difficult for Luke to see his mother so broken after the murder. Before Big John had been killed, Luke's mother had survived two bouts of breast cancer.

The first time she'd gotten it, it had been treated with radiation and chemo. She'd lost all her hair and had been sick for months. When it came back the second time, she'd had a double mastectomy. His father's death on top of everything else had nearly destroyed her.

"How's your mom doing as the new mayor?" Luke asked Chelsea.

"You know Stella—she's loving her newfound power and being the center of attention everywhere she goes," Chelsea replied. "It's what she's always wanted."

Stella Black owned the ranch next to the Kings' place. She was a tough lady who had single-handedly run her ranch and raised two children. Her first husband, the father of her son, Jacob, had died in a farm accident. He didn't know who Chelsea's father was.

Luke also knew there had been many times in the past when Chelsea had run to the King home after her mother had been particularly unkind to her. Stella always put on a pleasant face in public, but according to Chelsea, her mother could be a real witch behind closed doors.

"How's your brother doing, Chelsea?" he asked.

Luke had been friends with Chelsea's brother, Jacob, in high school, but Jacob had decided to leave Coyote Creek soon after graduation. He'd gone to Kansas City and worked as a police officer.

"He's doing fine. I think he's making plans to move back here in the next couple of weeks," she replied.

"Really? It would be great to have him back in town. Is he planning on joining the police force here?" Luke asked.

"I'm really not sure. I'm just glad he's coming home," Chelsea said.

"How's Carrie doing? You two seem thick as thieves," Johnny asked.

"Naturally, she's nervous about whoever is after her, but I have to say she's one of the strongest women I've ever known," Luke replied. "I'm picking her up later to go to the Red Barn."

"You guys seem to be hanging out there a lot," Johnny observed. "Do I need to worry about you developing a drinking problem?"

Luke laughed. "Not hardly. Carrie and I just enjoy having a few beers, listening to the music and just chilling," Luke replied. It was true. There were times when he was so deep in conversation with her that he momentarily forgot what they were really there for.

When they reached the big house, the air inside smelled of savory roast and simmering vegetables. His mother was seated in the wing-back chair next to the sofa. She wore a blue dressing gown that hung on her thin frame, and a blue-and-white scarf was wrapped around her head. Luke knew her hair was just starting to grow back in after the chemo treatments she'd undergone.

Despite the fact that she was far too thin and looked achingly fragile, Margaret King was still a beautiful woman. Her heart-shaped face showcased her bright blue eyes and her warm smiles.

Her eyes lit up when she saw him. "Luke, it's so nice to have you here for dinner. It's been a minute."

He walked over to her and kissed her on the cheek. "Sorry it's been a while since I've been here, but I'm looking forward to eating with you tonight."

"Are you still seeing Carrie?" she asked.

"I am."

She smiled. "I like her, Luke. I think she's a keeper."

Guilt swept through him. He was deceiving everyone by pretending he and Carrie were romantically involved. At that moment the door opened again, and Caleb walked in.

He greeted all of them and thankfully appeared to be relatively sober. "It's wonderful to have all my boys at the table tonight," Margaret said as they all moved into the dining room and sat down.

As always, the empty chair at the head of the table evoked a tightening in Luke's chest. His anger rose—anger that Big John wasn't in his chair where he belonged, anger that he was dead and they didn't know who had done it or why. More than anything Luke wanted to know why. What was the motive for killing such a good man?

"Where's Ashley tonight?" Luke asked. Since the murder his sister usually tried to come out and eat dinner with their mother.

"She had a lot of new items come in today, and she told me she wanted to log them into her inventory so she could get some of them out on the shelves by tomorrow," Margaret replied. "She said she'd try to get out here tomorrow night."

"And she didn't need your help?" Luke asked Chelsea. Chelsea had gotten a job in Ashley's shop a little over a month ago.

"Apparently not," Chelsea replied. "She didn't call me in to help her. But I do work tomorrow night, so she should be free to have dinner here."

Nellie Maddox appeared, carrying in steaming platters of food. Big John had hired Nellie to cook meals when Margaret had first been diagnosed with breast cancer. Since that time, Nellie had become part of the family. She was both the live-in cook and housekeeper.

Nellie was in her midsixties. She was a little bit chubby, with long gray hair that she wore in a tight bun at the nape of her neck. She also had kind brown eyes. She was not only an excellent cook, but she'd also become a confidante to Margaret.

Luke knew that often in the evenings Margaret and Nellie relaxed in the living room and watched television together. It was nice for him to know his mother wasn't all alone in the big house.

Tonight, for dinner, there were thick slices of roast and a platter of potatoes and carrots. Thick, rich gravy and homemade dinner rolls rounded out the meal. As they ate, Caleb was more talkative than Luke could ever remember.

When Big John was alive, Caleb rarely came to dinner, and if he did, he was usually silent and sullen. But tonight he appeared energized and was in a good mood. He also didn't appear to be drunk or drugged up.

As Luke remembered Carrie's assessment of Caleb's work, a heavy dread settled in his chest. There was no question that Big John had often ridden Caleb's ass hard, but Caleb had needed a firm hand. He'd been irresponsible and rebellious and often straight up disrespectful.

Still, Luke couldn't help but wonder if his father's killer was seated at the dinner table and not in the Red Barn. It was a sickening thought and one he hoped and prayed wasn't true, but he just didn't know.

As he listened to Caleb talk about his plans for

his art showing and Johnny and Chelsea laugh and joke about their wedding plans, it felt like an affront to the man who was absent from the table.

Dammit, Luke wanted to know why his father was gone. He wanted to know who had shot Big John twice in the driveway of his own home.

Was he the only one who had not been able to move on? Was he the only one in the whole damn family who felt the absolute need to put a killer behind bars before he could really move on with the rest of his life?

If he found out that Caleb had been responsible for Big John's death, then he would see to it that his brother was arrested and prosecuted for the crime.

It would destroy a big piece of his heart if Caleb was guilty. Despite their differences, Luke loved his younger brother, but the guilty party had to pay. And he was more determined than ever to find the person responsible for the empty chair at the table.

"I GOT TO go into town to get some groceries, and you know I got nobody to watch you," he said as he began to tape down the thin little arms. "You just be good, Billie. Be good while I'm gone and I'll buy you some of that banana food that you like. I'll be back here as soon as possible."

Billie mewled as if in protest. "Don't whine,"

he snapped. "You know how much I hate it when you whine. Use your words, Billie."

God, he was so damned aggravated. And it was all *her* fault. As he continued to tape down Billie's arms, he thought about his last attempt to kill Carrie.

He'd almost had her. He'd managed to wreck her car, and it had all been so perfect. Eventually, if he'd had some more time, he would have found the bitch wherever she'd hidden and put a bullet in her head. He'd been close…so achingly close to achieving his goal.

But she'd been saved by another vehicle showing up. Damn his bad luck. The last thing he'd wanted was for whoever was in the other truck to be able to identify him. And damn her good luck in that other truck showing up just in time to save her.

His rage toward her was now all-consuming. Killing her was the first thing he thought about in the morning and the last thing he thought about before going to sleep. The only way to rid himself of the rage that burned inside him was to take her off the face of the earth forever.

He needed to watch her die, slowly and painfully. She deserved to die for all the lies she'd told, lies that had destroyed his entire life. He finished taping Billie down. "Okay, I'll be home as soon as possible."

The mewling came again. "Dammit, Billie, stop whining. You know I have to tape you down to make sure you stay safe while I'm gone. I have to get some groceries. You want to eat, don't you? I told you I'll be back as soon as I can."

He grabbed his wallet and his keys from the edge of the kitchen table and then headed out the front door, locking it behind him. Thankfully there was very little damage to the front of his truck. Hell, the old truck was beaten up and damaged on nearly all four sides anyway. Nobody would even notice a few more dents and bangs.

There was no way anyone would know he was the one after her. It had been nearly a year since she'd told him all the lies. He'd been patient, but now his patience was gone, and it was time for her to pay.

There was only one thing he really regretted. He was sorry he'd spoken to her when he was hunting her down in the moments after the wreck. He hadn't worried about her hearing his voice then, because he believed he was going to kill her.

Apparently—thankfully—she hadn't recognized his voice, because nobody had shown up at his door to arrest him. If he was going to rid himself of the constant anger inside him, he had to kill her. He just had to get more creative in how he intended to complete his goal. He could do that.

He smiled to himself as he pulled into a parking space in front of the grocery store. He knew he could come up with the perfect plan to assure that bitch's demise. It was just a matter of time.

Chapter Eight

Carrie sat at the kitchen table with Emily. The two of them had gotten home from work a half an hour before and were now sharing a frozen pizza for dinner.

It had been a good day. Dr. Morris, who was much older than Dr. Holloway, had been married to his wife for thirty years. He was an infinitely kind man both as a doctor and as an employer.

"It was so nice to work today and not feel like I had to dodge and weave inappropriate closeness and touches from the doctor," Carrie said.

"I've been working for Dr. Morris for four years now, and there has never been an issue like that." Emily moved a second piece of pizza from the pizza stone in the center of the table to her plate.

"I didn't realize just how much I dreaded going into work each morning until now," Carrie admitted.

"I'm glad you're with Dr. Morris. He truly is

a good guy to work for. All the staff absolutely love him."

"I'm glad I'm working for him now, too," Carrie replied.

"So, what are your plans for the rest of the night?" Emily asked.

"The usual—Luke is picking me up around seven thirty, and we're heading to the Red Barn to hang out."

Emily eyed her closely and with more than a bit of concern. "Are you sure you really should be doing that right now? Surely it would be safer to stay here or at Luke's place."

"If you're concerned about my safety, don't be. Luke is a well-armed bodyguard, and I feel perfectly safe when I'm with him."

"So, what's going on between the two of you?"

"What do you mean?" Carrie took a bite of the pizza.

"I mean, you two have been seeing each other every night for a while now. What's going on with the relationship? Where's your head where he's concerned?"

Carrie swallowed her bite and then took a drink of her soda before replying. "I'm in love with him." The words popped out of her mouth as her heart expanded with warmth. She knew with every fiber of her being that she was hopelessly, madly in love with Luke King.

"Oh Carrie, that makes me happy for you and worried about you at the same time."

"Worried why?" Carrie looked at her friend in confusion.

"Before he was dating you, he had quite a reputation as a heartbreaker. I don't want him to break your heart, too."

Carrie laughed. "Trust me, I'm not a bit worried about that. Has Luke dated a lot of women in the past? Absolutely. But all he was doing was looking for somebody he wanted to spend the rest of his life with. We talked about it, and I'm fine about it."

"Do you think you're that somebody for him?" Emily asked. "Are you the person he wants to spend his life with?"

"I hope I am." She desperately wanted to be that somebody in his life forever.

Emily picked a piece of pepperoni off her pizza and popped it into her mouth. "So, has he told you he's in love with you?"

Carrie frowned thoughtfully. "No, we haven't said the words to each other, but I believe he is. I feel it, Em. I feel his love for me in everything he does."

"Have you slept with him yet?"

Carrie felt the warmth that leaped into her cheeks.

Emily laughed. "You don't even have to answer

that. It's written all over your face." She sobered. "I just hope you don't get hurt, Carrie."

Carrie released a dry laugh. "I've got some crazy monster trying to kill me. Right now, I'm not too worried about Luke hurting me."

"Point taken." Emily's eyes darkened. "And you still haven't figured out who the voice belongs to?"

Carrie shook her head. "I've absolutely racked my brain, and I still can't figure it out." It was so frustrating, because she knew if she could identify whom the voice belonged to, then Lane could make an arrest and she would no longer have to fear for her life. "It's like having something on the tip of your tongue but not being able to figure out what it is."

"Well, I hope you figure it out sooner rather than later," Emily replied. "Just so you know… I would definitely beat somebody's butt if they came after you and I was anywhere around."

Carrie laughed and then smiled at her friend. "Thanks, Emily."

At seven thirty as she waited for Luke to arrive to pick her up, she thought about how much she appreciated Emily's friendship.

They had known each other in school, but Emily was two years older than Carrie, so they hadn't hung out together then. They'd reconnected and become close friends when they were working together at the hospital. That had been five years ago, and their friendship had only grown deeper and better over those years.

Emily knew her better than anyone else except for Luke. Emily had been by her side when she'd broken up with Rory. She knew all the things Carrie longed for in her life. More than anything, Carrie wanted a family. Losing her mother at such a young age had shortchanged her in the family department.

She wanted to build what she had lost when her mother had passed away—a family unit with a husband who loved her and children she could cherish.

When she saw Luke pull up in the driveway, her first instinct was to run out the door to greet him, but instead she remained inside, knowing he'd come up to get her and escort her to his truck.

Twilight had fallen, heavy and dark with purple shadows. She watched him get out of his truck, his hand on the butt of his gun as he looked to the left and then to the right.

Since the night of the wreck, the only place she truly felt safe was in Luke's presence. She knew when they were together, he was constantly looking out for her safety.

When he reached her front door, she opened it and stepped outside. "Hi," she said.

"Hi, yourself," he replied lightly. "Are you ready for another night at our favorite spot?"

"I'm ready." When they reached the truck, he opened the passenger door, and she slid inside and then watched as he walked around to the driver's door.

He looked as handsome as ever with his slightly shaggy dark hair complementing the bright blue of his eyes. As usual, he wore jeans that fit perfectly on his long legs and across his nice butt. He wore a light blue T-shirt that stretched taut across his broad shoulders and chest and made her remember stroking her hands across his naked body.

Her love for him buoyed up in her chest, making her feel half-giddy. Did he love her? Or was he just using her in the capacity she'd given him permission to do? Surely he had feelings for her after all the time they had spent together.

He got into the truck, and she shoved her thoughts out of her mind. Now wasn't the place or time to tell him she'd fallen in love with him— hard.

"So, tell me all about your first day of work," he said as they pulled away from her house.

"It was actually a great day," she replied and went on to tell him everything she had experienced with her new boss. By the time she finished, they had reached the Red Barn.

As always, they took the table closest to Peter and his cohorts, who already appeared more than a little bit buzzed. "Hey look, lover boy is back,"

Peter said, and the men at his table all guffawed as Carrie and Luke sat down.

Carrie immediately felt the tension that wafted off Luke. "I'd rather be a lover boy than a killer," Luke replied.

The laughter halted, and Peter glared at Luke, his dark eyes intense. "And just who the hell do you think I killed?" The air around them suddenly snapped with a whisper of danger.

"I believe you shot my father," Luke replied.

Carrie held her breath. She'd had no idea that Luke had intended to confront Peter openly this way. There was a moment of pregnant silence, and then Peter threw back his head and laughed.

"Now why in the hell would I kill Big John?" Peter asked.

"I think your boss hired you to do it. He knew my dad was going to win the mayoral election, so he wanted Dad out of the way," Luke replied.

Peter narrowed his eyes. "You're way out of line here, man. First of all, there's no amount of money that would make me murder somebody. Secondly, Wayne Bridges is the tightest man in the world. He wouldn't part with a dime of his money for a scheme like that. I might be a drunk, and some might think I'm a lowlife, but I'm not a damned murderer, and you better not be going around and saying I am."

"I'm not saying anything to anybody." Luke got

up from the table and looked at him. "But let's be real here—you're one of only a very few here in town who could have made that shot."

"You got that right," Peter fired back. "There's only a few of us who could have made that shot, and if I remember right, you three King boys are all good shots, too. Maybe you fired that shot, Luke."

Luke lunged across the table, and Peter jumped up from his chair. "Take that back," Luke shouted as his hands curled into fists at his side.

Carrie's chest tightened with wild anxiety. Luke's anger was a palpable force in the air. But if a fight broke out, she knew he wouldn't just be fighting Peter—he'd be fighting all the men were with Peter.

"Luke," she said, hoping her voice would reach him through his haze of emotion.

However, he remained in fight mode and glaring at Peter. "You take that back," he repeated angrily.

"I was just making a point," Peter said. "There are plenty of people who could have made that shot. I'm not the only one, and I had nothing to do with your daddy's death." He sat back down at his table. "And that's the damned honest truth."

Slowly Luke's fists uncurled, and he drew several deep, audible breaths. He turned and looked at Carrie. "I'll be right back with our drinks."

She watched him weave toward the bar through the small crowd of people. She released a shuddery sigh. She'd been sure there was going to be a fistfight.

There was no question Peter had been a jerk to say what he had said. And Luke had taken his bait, responding in anger. She didn't know how Luke felt about the conversation, but she believed Peter.

As much as she'd hoped their little scheme would work to get the closure Luke needed, she no longer believed Peter was behind Big John's murder.

Luke returned with two beers, and for the next half an hour or so they sat. Luke was quiet, obviously deep in his own thoughts, and she didn't know what to say or how to pull him out and up. For the first time since meeting him, she didn't know what to say to him, and she couldn't imagine what he was thinking.

"Are you ready to go?" he asked once their beers were gone.

"I'm ready if you are," she replied.

Together they got up and headed for the exit. The night was warmer than usual, and Luke immediately turned on the truck air conditioner.

"Talk to me, Luke," she finally said after several minutes of driving in silence.

He released a deep, audible sigh. "I'm totally ashamed of myself."

"What?" She looked at him in surprise. "Why?"

"I'm ashamed of how quickly I lost my temper in there. I'm ashamed of how far I allowed Peter to get under my skin."

"What Peter said was totally out of line," she replied firmly.

"Still, I shouldn't have responded to him in the way I did. I know he's a jerk, but that doesn't mean I have to be one, too." He flashed her a quick, contrite look. "Sorry about that."

"You don't have to apologize to me. I know how emotions run high around this particular topic." She was oddly pleased with his apology, even though she didn't think he owed her one.

"Now I don't know whether I believe Peter or not." He tapped his fingers on the steering wheel. "There's a part of me that wants to believe he was lying. I mean, why should I believe he'd tell me the truth about committing a murder?"

"I don't know what to believe," she replied. "But he certainly sounded like he was telling the truth. Maybe what you need to do is make a list of all the people in town who are excellent shots with a rifle."

"Yeah, that's definitely a good idea," he replied. "I don't know why I didn't think of that sooner. I just homed in on Peter from the very beginning and that was that."

He drove for a few minutes in silence, and she

could feel the weight of his thoughts—thoughts she wished she could see. She wanted to support him in any way she could, but she couldn't do that if he didn't share with her. And at the moment he wasn't sharing.

It was only when he pulled up and parked in front of her house that he turned to look at her, his tension-filled features clear in the light from the dashboard. "You know what really stinks?"

"What's that?" She reached out and placed her hand on his forearm. She could feel his muscles there were all bunched and knotted. His eyes looked positively feverish in the pale illumination.

"I *need* Peter to be guilty. I *need* to believe he's the one who killed my dad, otherwise I'm left with only one other suspect, and that's my brother."

He stared at her bleakly, and in that moment her heart absolutely broke for him. "Luke, have you considered the possibility that it isn't Peter or Caleb, but your father's killer might be somebody else who is not even on your radar?"

He frowned. "Dammit, Carrie, how am I supposed to solve this if it's somebody else? I don't know who else to look at for this."

"Luke, it's not your job to solve it," she replied gently.

"But it is," he said with a touch of anger. "It is my job, because nobody else cares about solving it. I have to do it to…to prove to my father that

I am worthy of his love...that I am the son who loves him most."

"Luke, your dad is dead," she said softly. "He won't care who solves his murder. I'm sure your dad knew how very much you loved him, and you don't have to prove your worthiness to him or anyone else. And I'm sure your father loved you very much."

He stared outside the front window. "I know he's dead and he won't care who solves his murder, but I won't stop digging until the killer is found out and thrown in jail. I'll go home and write up that list you suggested." He turned and looked at her, his gaze intent. "Carrie, are you still with me?"

"Of course. I'm with you for as long as you want me," she replied. Her love for him begged to be released. She wanted to tell him the depth of love she had for him in her heart, but she knew this wasn't the time—not when they were talking about murder.

Once again, he released a deep sigh that seemed to alleviate some of the anger that had gripped him. "I still want you," he replied. "Now let's get you inside." He opened his truck door and got out.

I still want you. His words shot a delectable warmth from her head to her toes. She knew he meant he still wanted her to help him solve his father's murder. She just hoped he still wanted her because he was falling in love with her.

LUKE SAT IN one of the chairs on his front porch and stared off to where the sun was slowly sinking in the sky, painting it in shades of fiery reds and oranges.

He'd called Carrie earlier in the day to tell her he wasn't going to the Red Barn tonight and he'd see her in the next day or two.

There was no question that his confrontation with Peter the night before had messed with his head. He had been so sure the man was guilty. Of course, Peter would be a fool to admit that he pulled the trigger and had killed Big John. But Peter's voice had rung with more than a grain of truth.

Surely if Bridges had paid Peter to kill a man, Lane would have checked out the finances between the two men. Apparently, there had been no flow of money between Wayne Bridges and Peter. Unless of course it had been cash and Peter was now sleeping on a pillow full of money that he couldn't deposit in any bank.

But what if it wasn't Peter? After he'd taken Carrie home the night before, he'd returned to his house and spent the next hour or so writing down the names of all the people he knew were more than proficient with a rifle.

Every couple of years, there was a shooting competition out at Walt Zimmerman's ranch. Walt was in his midsixties and had been hosting the contest for the past twenty years. Targets were set up in his pasture, and people paid a fee to participate. There were usually some out-of-town people who showed up, hoping to win first-place bragging rights and the five-hundred-dollar prize money.

Luke had stayed up half the night thinking of all the names of the men and women who had been able to hit close to the bull's-eye. Peter had been right in that all the King brothers were good shots.

He didn't know the names of the out-of-towners who showed up, but he'd been able to list a dozen people right here in town. There were even two women who had made the list. Henrietta Bakersfield worked at the post office. She was a mild-mannered woman, but put a rifle in her hand and she became Annie Oakley. The other woman who made his list was their esteemed mayor, Stella Black.

However, he couldn't think of a single motive that anyone on the list would have to kill Big John. So, he was back to square one, still thinking that Peter was good for the crime.

He now looked up the lane, where Caleb and Leroy stood outside the barn drinking beers and laughing. He knew Leroy now worked on the Black ranch, which made it easy for him to walk here to hang out with Caleb when Leroy was off duty. He stared at his brother for several long moments.

Was it Caleb? Had he somehow snapped, or had he been high and decided to take out his own father? Luke had heard his brother and his father fight the night before the murder.

Caleb had wanted Big John to give him the money to open up a place in town for Caleb to sell his artwork. Big John had laughed in his face and told Caleb if he wanted money, then he needed to get off his butt and do some work around the ranch, that he could earn the money, but Big John wasn't going to just give it to him.

Caleb had stormed out of the house, as angry as Luke had ever seen him. Had that fight prompted Caleb to get drunk or high and then seek out revenge? The very thought made Luke sick to his stomach.

Luke had never felt as alone as he did at this moment. He knew he could call Carrie and she'd be up for spending time with him, but he didn't feel like he'd be good company for her or anyone else at this moment in time.

He watched as Caleb and Leroy finished their beers and then headed up the path that would take them into the woods. It was an odd time to go hiking in the wooded area, but then again, maybe Caleb wanted to photograph some of the flowers he found at sunset.

What if Carrie was right? What if the killer was somebody not even on his radar? What if he never found the murderer? Would he be able to live the rest of his life with this yawning emptiness in his heart? Would he forever feel as if he'd somehow let his father down? There was definitely a part of him that was just tired of thinking of it all.

He got up from the chair and walked toward the big house. He suddenly felt the need to talk to his mother. He hadn't talked to her privately since before the murder, but he felt the need to do so now.

He found his mother seated in her chair in the great room. She brightened as he walked in. "Luke," she said in surprise.

"Do you have a minute?" he asked.

"Honey, I always have more than a minute for you. Please, sit down."

He sank down in the wing-back chair across from her.

She frowned. "What's going on, Luke? You look like you have a lot on your mind."

"I do," he admitted. He hesitated a moment and looked down at the coffee table. He drew a deep breath and then looked back at his mother. "I miss him, and I know you must miss him terribly, too. How do you get through each day?"

"Oh, Luke. I'm going to miss him every minute of every day for the rest of my life. But I have so many wonderful memories of him and of us together."

"But aren't you angry?" Luke pressed. "Don't you want revenge?"

"What good would revenge or anger do at this point? No matter how angry I am, that doesn't bring him back." She smiled at him gently. "And Luke, your anger won't bring him back, either."

"Logically I know that, but I feel like I need to keep searching for his killer so he'll know how much I loved him." Luke's voice broke as a wave of emotion gripped him.

Margaret got out of her chair and moved to the sofa, then gestured for him to join her there. Once he was seated next to her, she took his hands in hers.

"Luke, your father knew how much you loved him, and he loved you very much. He used to talk to me about how much he enjoyed it when it was just the two of you in the stables. He thought you were so bright, so knowledgeable about the horses."

"I... I never knew that," Luke replied.

"Johnny demanded your father's attention. He was so bold, and Caleb...well, your daddy didn't understand Caleb at all. Caleb demanded all negative attention. But you...you were quieter and didn't demand much of anything. Your dad actually admired that about you. He thought you were much stronger than both Johnny and Caleb. Oh Luke, he was so proud of you."

Tears burned at Luke's eyes as his emotions bubbled over. "That's all I ever wanted...to make him proud of me." To his horror a sob ripped out from deep within him.

"Oh, honey." Margaret wrapped her arms tightly around him, and suddenly he was bawling like a baby in his mother's arms. They were the first tears he had cried for his father.

He sobbed for the days he would never have again, for the laughter he'd never again share with his father. He cried because he didn't understand why such a good man had been killed.

"Tell me, how do we go on?" he finally managed to choke out.

Margaret patted him on the back. "We go on because Big John made us all strong, and he would want us to go on and live our best lives. We go on by remembering the laughter we all shared, the love he shared with us. We honor him when we remember him, Luke, not when we harbor anger and a desire for revenge in our hearts."

Luke finally sat up and wiped at his eyes, embarrassed by his breakdown in front of his mother. "God, I don't remember the last time that I cried like that."

"I remember the last time you did." She smiled at him. "It was when you were twelve years old and Melody Watkins didn't give you a valentine."

Luke laughed. "I had decided I was going to

grow up and marry Melody, and then she broke my heart by not giving me a valentine."

"Speaking of your heart, how are you and Carrie getting along?"

"We're doing fine." He still hated that he was lying to his mother about the relationship.

"Is it a true love connection? You know I'd love to see you settle down with a wife. I'm more than ready for some grandbabies."

"Whoa, slow down," he said and laughed again. "It's not like that with us. We're just really good friends."

"That's the way it started with me and your father. I considered him my very best friend, and he felt the same way about me. Then one day we realized we never wanted to be apart from each other and what we really felt for each other was actually a deep, abiding love."

"I don't know where things are going between me and Carrie. We're just taking it one day at a time right now," he replied.

"As long as you're both on the same page," Margaret said. "You're such a good man, Luke. Don't let your father's death stop you from living your life to the fullest. That's what he would want for you."

Fifteen minutes later as Luke walked back toward his place, he felt lighter than he had since his father's death. He was embarrassed by his blubbering in his mother's arms, but it had definitely been cathartic.

Still, nothing had changed in his desire to find his father's killer, although the need to do so was a little less pressing. And now that some of the pressure was momentarily gone, his worries about Carrie filled him.

When would the creep who was after her be found out? He worried every day when he knew she was driving to and from work. It soothed him most days that she and Emily could ride together to work, but their work schedules would not always be the same.

He wished like hell she could identify the person behind the voice, but so far, she couldn't... just like he couldn't identify his father's murderer.

He had just passed the barn when Leroy and Caleb came running out of the woods. They ran like they were being chased by demons out of hell.

They whirled into the barn and slammed the door behind them. A minute later another man came crashing out of the woods. He was a short, wiry man with dark hair tied back at the nape of his neck with a long leather tie. Tattoos covered his face and neck. He was missing one eye, and he held a gun in his hand. Luke immediately pulled his weapon, and for several long moments the two faced each other in a standoff.

"Who are you and what are you doing on our

property?" Luke asked. Luke had never seen this man before. He wasn't a native of Coyote Creek. His heart quickened as he faced off with the stranger. What in the hell was going on here?

"You don't need to know my name." The man held his gun steady and pointed at Luke's chest. Luke returned the favor by keeping his gun aimed at the man.

The air snapped with danger as the two men faced off. Luke had no idea what was going on, but his entire body filled with adrenaline. "I need to know what you're doing on my property," Luke said. He narrowed his eyes as he watched the man closely.

Was he going to shoot? Who was this man and what was he doing here? Luke held his gun tightly, ready to pull the trigger if necessary.

After several long moments, the stranger lowered his gun and put it in the black holster that rode low on his hips. "I'm looking for Caleb King. I know he just came this way."

Luke slowly lowered his gun but kept it firmly in his hand. "Why are you looking for him?"

"I got some business with him."

Luke narrowed his eyes. "What kind of business?"

"None of your business," the man replied sharply. "Are you going to tell me where he went or not?"

"I'm not Caleb's keeper. I don't know where

he went, but I know it's time for you to get off our property. Otherwise, I'll call the cops to get you off."

"Hey, I don't want any problems here." The man took several steps backward. "There's no need to get the cops involved. If you see Caleb, just tell him Joker is looking for him and will catch up with him later." The man turned and ran back the way he had come, disappearing into the falling night shadows.

Luke stared after him for several long moments. What in the hell was that all about? That guy didn't exactly look like an upstanding citizen, and he definitely hadn't wanted any cop involvement. The man had looked like a tough thug.

What business could Caleb have with a person like that? What on earth had his brother gotten himself into? And was it possible it hadn't been Caleb who had killed their father? Was it possible it was somebody Caleb was doing "business" with?

Chapter Nine

Carrie had been disappointed when Luke called to tell her he was taking a night off from the Red Barn, which meant he was taking a night off from her.

However, it had worked out well, for her father had been in town, and so she'd spent the evening catching up with him. As she'd talked with her father about all things big and small, she'd thought about Luke, who would never again have a chance to just sit and talk with his father. Her heart hurt for Luke and his loss.

When it was time to say goodbye, she hugged her father extra hard, recognizing that he could be taken from her in the blink of an eye. The death of Big John had reminded her that everyone was living on borrowed time and it was important to tell the people in her life that she loved them whenever she got the chance.

Today work had been as pleasant as the day be-

fore. She and Emily had picked up Chinese food
for dinner on the way home, and then Luke had
called to ask her if he could pick her up around
six thirty.

There was something in his voice that made her
feel like he needed her. He hadn't mentioned going
to the Red Barn, but she wanted to do whatever
he needed to do.

At six fifteen dinner had been cleared up and
she'd freshened up and changed from her scrubs
into a pair of jeans and a sleeveless hot-pink
blouse.

She sat on the sofa awaiting Luke's arrival, and
as always when she had a moment to think, her
thoughts went to the dark place of knowing somebody wanted her dead. Who did that voice be-
long to?

Had she heard it in town? Maybe somebody
working at the grocery store or in one of the other
stores she frequented? Had he been a patient of
Dr. Holloway's practice? Or had one of his family members been in Dr. Holloway's office and she
had been the attending nurse?

She got up from the sofa and moved to the front
window to watch for Luke. She appreciated that
he was a punctual man, and at precisely six thirty
he pulled into the driveway.

As usual, he got out and she waited until he
was at her front door before opening it. "I missed

seeing you last night," he said once they were in the truck.

"I missed seeing you, too," she replied, warmed by his words. She decided not to tell him that she'd spent the evening before with her father. There was no reason for him to know that, and it would only rub salt in his wounds. "So, how was your night?" she asked.

"Both soothing and disturbing."

"Those words don't exactly go together," she replied.

He flashed her a quick smile. "Yeah, I know." The grin was quickly swallowed up by a frown. "On the soothing side, I had a really good talk with my mother. She told me not only how much my dad loved me, but that he enjoyed the time he spent in the stables when it was just him and me."

"That's good, Luke. I hope you took her words to heart," she replied.

"I did. In fact, yesterday with her was the first time I really grieved, and now I feel like a big weight has been lifted off me."

She was happy for him. It was what he'd desperately needed, and now maybe he would be ready to move on with the rest of his life…be ready to move on with her.

"However, I still intend to hunt for his killer," he added, making her feel like he wasn't ready to move on at all. It definitely disappointed her a bit.

"So, does that mean we're headed back to the Red Barn tonight?"

"Not tonight," he said. "Tonight I just wanted to hang out with you."

"You know I always love spending time with you, Luke."

He was silent for a few minutes, and then he flashed her a quick glance. "We're friends, right?"

"Absolutely. I consider you one of my very best friends," she replied.

"Good, so we're both on the same page with that."

"Definitely." Was he intentionally friend zoning her, or did he just want to make sure she truly was his friend? She wasn't sure what his words meant, and she was afraid to ask him to make himself clearer.

He pulled up in front of his place and parked. "Why don't I grab us a couple of beers and we can sit on the front porch for a while?" he said as they walked to his door.

"That sounds good to me, and then you're going to tell me the disturbing part of your day yesterday." She sank down in the cushion of one of the porch chairs.

"Definitely. I'll be right back." He disappeared into the house.

It was a beautiful evening. The late-June sun was warm but not too warm as a light breeze blew.

The breeze rustled in the leaves of the nearby trees, and birds chirped their happy songs, making a pleasant melody of nature.

Luke came back out the door with two beers. He handed her one, and then he sank down in the chair next to her. "By the way, you look really nice," he said.

"Thanks." He looked as good as ever in his jeans and a striped gray-and-white polo shirt.

He took a long draw from his beer and then released a deep sigh and looked off in the distance. A muscle ticked in his jaw, and she could feel a new intensity wafting off him.

"Talk to me, Luke. What's going on? What has you so disturbed?"

It was then he told her about the man who had been chasing down Caleb the night before. "Did you speak to Caleb about it?" she asked when he was finished.

"I spoke to him this afternoon. He insisted that he had no idea a man was chasing him and Leroy the night before and that he didn't know anyone named Joker."

"Did you believe him?"

"No. It was obvious he and Leroy were running back to the barn for a reason. They were running away from this Joker guy."

"So, what do you think is going on?" she asked.

He stared off toward the barn for a long moment and then looked back at her. "I might be jumping to conclusions due to the way this Joker looked, but I think it was maybe some sort of a drug deal gone wrong." Once again, he gazed off into the distance.

"Then you think your brother is into hard drugs?" she asked.

He turned and looked at her. "Hell, Carrie, I don't know what else to think. And now I'm thinking maybe Caleb had nothing to do with Dad's death, but maybe some low-life drug dealer that Caleb brought into his life killed him."

"So, are you going to take this all to Lane?"

He looked down at his feet and then took a drink of his beer, remaining silent for several moments. "I don't know what I'm going to do yet. I've been thinking about what to do all last night and today. I need to talk to Johnny about it, but he left early this morning for Oklahoma City. Some rancher there is auctioning off all his cattle and horses, and Johnny wanted to take a look at them. He won't be home until tomorrow afternoon, so I have to wait to talk to him until then."

"What does your gut instinct tell you to do?" she asked.

"I know how my father would want to handle it. He'd want to keep everything in the family. If

Caleb is doing hard drugs, then he doesn't need to be hounded by Lane about a murder. What he does need is some sort of an intervention. As a family, we need to see if we can get him into treatment."

"Yes, but don't you also need to tell Lane that it's possible some druggie lowlifes might have killed your father?"

The muscle in his jaw pulsated once again. "I intend to find this Joker guy myself and have a little chat with him about my father's murder."

Carrie gasped. "Oh Luke, please don't do that. Listening to Peter in the Red Barn and hoping for a confession is one thing, but this is something much different—something much more dangerous."

"I still have to chase this down, Carrie. I *have* to. It might be the only way I get some answers and some closure in this whole mess."

She placed her beer on the small table, got out of her chair and knelt next to him. She reached out and grabbed hold of his arm and held on tightly. "Luke, if you pursue this, then I fear that the closure you'll get will be your own death. Please take this all to Lane. You don't have to mention Caleb's name. Just tell him about this creep lurking around your property. Leave this Joker guy alone."

"I'll take it to Lane when I know more, and only after Johnny and I decide to," he replied firmly.

Her heart raced with fear for him. If what he

believed was true, then this Joker person was a drug dealer, and not the garden-variety kind who sold weed to his friends. Just from the way Luke had described the man, he sounded like he might be a hardened criminal.

True, she was doing something she'd always hated—she was judging a book by its cover. But given the circumstances, it was hard not to believe the one-eyed Joker with facial tattoos was a dope dealer and a criminal.

"But maybe this man is already wanted for something else," she continued, desperate to change Luke's mind about going after the man himself. She released her hold on his arm and returned to her chair. "If you'd take this to Lane, he might have the resources to hunt the man down."

"I told you this is something I have to do," he snapped, his tone immediately hurting her feelings. He raked a hand through his hair and shook his head. "God, I'm sorry, Carrie. I didn't mean to come at you like that. You're the last person in the world who deserves any of my anger."

"I accept your apology," she replied. She knew how high his emotions were at the moment. "But I can't help but be afraid for you, Luke. This driving need you have to find your father's killer is now taking you into what I consider very dangerous territory."

Once again, she wanted to tell him she was in love with him, but she didn't want to have that conversation in the midst of a talk about drug dealers and murder. And so she held her emotions in check. But sooner or later she was going to have to speak of her love for him.

If she wasn't killed by the man who had tried to kill her before, then she feared she'd die a different kind of death if Luke didn't love her back.

IT WAS THE next evening when Luke finally sat down with his older brother to tell him everything that had happened with Caleb. Just after dinner, Luke sat on the sofa in Johnny's house. Chelsea sat next to him, and Johnny was in his recliner.

Johnny's house had originally been the old foreman's cabin. He'd spent four years renovating the place and had turned it into a really beautiful home.

"How was the trip to Oklahoma?" Luke asked.

"It was a total bust," Johnny replied. "The horses were old nags, and the cattle looked even worse. All the equipment was old and rusty. There was absolutely nothing there for us."

"That's a shame," Luke replied.

"It was a pleasant drive and we stayed in a nice hotel for the night, so it wasn't a total bust." Chelsea shot a warm smile to Johnny.

Johnny laughed. "She thought the drive was nice because she had me trapped in the truck to discuss wedding plans."

"And what are the plans?" Luke asked and realized he was putting off discussing the real issue he'd come to talk about.

"We're planning on getting married in early September, and I just want a small gathering in the pasture where there's an old wagon on my mother's land," Chelsea said, her eyes shining brightly.

"What's so important about that wagon?" Luke knew which one she was talking about. It was a broken-down old wagon right along the property line between the Black land and the Kings' land.

"It's the place where I realized I was still in love with Johnny," she said.

"And the same is true for me," Johnny replied.

"September is only a few months away. Don't most people take a year or so to plan a wedding?" Luke asked.

"Johnny and I don't want a big to-do, so we should easily be able to pull together what I want in a short amount of time," Chelsea replied.

Johnny looked back at Luke. "So, what's up with you? You normally don't just pop in to visit."

Luke told his brother about the encounter with Joker. When he was finished, a grim frown cut across Johnny's forehead. "So, you're thinking maybe this Joker guy killed Dad over a drug deal with Caleb?" he asked.

"It's a thought," Luke replied.

"Luke, think about it. Why would a drug dealer kill the money man? Everybody knew that the only way Caleb got money was from Dad," Johnny said.

Luke frowned thoughtfully. He hadn't thought about that, but Johnny was right. It didn't make any sense for Joker to have killed Big John. Dammit, he'd been so sure he was onto something.

"What we really need to talk about is what we intend to do about Caleb," Johnny said.

"He obviously needs some help," Chelsea said. "He's needed help for some time."

"Definitely," Johnny agreed. "Do you want to take this all to Lane?"

"I don't know. I don't want to throw Caleb under the bus if the only thing he's guilty of is doing drugs. Maybe we should get everyone together, Mom and Ashley included, and have some sort of a family intervention."

"It sounds like he definitely needs treatment. I'll do some research tonight and see what kind of in-house treatment facility we can get him into," Johnny said.

"So, maybe we can plan this for Sunday afternoon," Luke said. "That gives you all day tomorrow to be able to come up with someplace for him."

"Then why don't we all meet at around three o'clock? Mom can make sure Caleb shows up," Johnny replied.

"And I can work for Ashley so she can be here," Chelsea added.

"I just hope with all of us on the same page, Caleb will agree to get help," Luke said. He wanted his brother to reach his full potential, and Caleb couldn't do that with all the drinking he did or whatever drugs he was taking.

A half an hour later as he walked back to his place, he thought about what Johnny had said about Joker. Johnny might not believe that Joker would kill Big John, but he might have killed Big John as some sort of a warning to Caleb.

A headache tightened across Luke's forehead with nauseating intensity. Too many thoughts were crowding his brain. When he got to his house, he sank down in his recliner and closed his eyes.

Immediately a vision of Carrie filled his brain, and he felt himself relaxing. That's what she brought to him—a kind of peace no other woman had ever given him before.

He would have spent this evening with her, but she'd had a late night working at the hospital. She was supposed to get off at eight o'clock. Emily wouldn't be with her, so Luke intended to be in the parking lot to follow her home.

His family might be falling apart, but he was determined not to let Carrie down. Until the creep who was after her was behind bars, he would do whatever he could to keep her safe from harm.

It was Sunday afternoon when all of the King family came together for the intervention. While they waited for Caleb to arrive, Margaret sat on the sofa. She appeared worried about confronting her youngest son. Ashley displayed a bad case of nerves by prattling about the latest inventory at her shop. Johnny looked grim and determined, and Luke just wanted to get it all over with.

He still found it heartbreaking to think that it was possible his brother was in any way responsible for Big John's death, but whether possible or not, he knew Caleb definitely needed help.

Luke still wanted to find out more about this Joker fellow and what role he might have in Caleb's life and Big John's murder. He still felt a burning need to solve his father's murder, but over the last couple of days, he'd just been tired.

He'd just been tired of thinking about murder and mayhem. He was exhausted by spending so long twisting and turning things around in his head. He told himself he just needed a night or two off—a night or two to rest his mind, and then he'd get back to things stronger than ever.

More importantly, while he believed Carrie supported him, over the past few days he'd sensed her growing impatience with his quest. The last thing he wanted to do was push her out of his life. She was far too important to him as a friend.

The room fell silent as Caleb walked in. "Mom told me there was some kind of a family meeting and I needed to be here," he said and sat down next to their mother on the sofa. "I hope you've all decided to back me in my art endeavors and we're here because you're all going to give me the seed money I need to open up a storefront."

"That's not why we're all here," Johnny said, obviously taking the lead.

"Then why are we here?" Caleb asked curiously.

"We're here for you, Caleb," Ashley said.

Caleb's eyes narrowed, and he visibly tensed as he looked at each and every one of them. "So, what exactly is going on here?"

"We all think you need help, Caleb," Johnny said. "You're drinking too much, and we know you're doing drugs."

"Are you wearing your daddy hat now, Johnny?" Caleb asked irritably. "He was always accusing me of doing all kinds of drugs."

"Are you, Caleb?" Margaret asked, her voice

soft and filled with concern. "Are you doing all kinds of drugs?" She looked at him worriedly.

"No, Ma, I'm not. I like beer, and I'll admit I like smoking a joint now and then, but that's the only drug I do," Caleb replied. "It's not a big deal that I like weed. Smoking helps me open my mind for my painting."

"Then how do you explain Joker?" Luke asked.

"I can't," Caleb said. "I have no idea who Joker is or why he was supposedly looking for me." Once again, he looked at everyone in the room. "Is this one of those interventions? Is that why you are all here?"

"I do have some information here about a great place in Kentucky," Johnny said. He reached for a handful of papers he'd carried in with him and had placed on the end table. "It's a nice place, Caleb, and they use art as a form of therapy. I think it would be good for you to get away from the ranch for a couple of months and just work on yourself."

"You've got to be kidding me. Wow. I thought my family couldn't betray me any more, but I guess I was wrong," Caleb replied in obvious ir-rritation.

"Oh, Caleb, honey. We all just want the best for you," Margaret said.

"You, of all people are breaking my heart right now," Caleb said to Margaret. "I thought you understood me. All I want is seed money to open a store. Why can't you just do that and then leave me alone?"

Margaret dabbed at her eyes with a tissue.

"Caleb, this is what's best for you," Johnny said authoritatively. "We all want you to thrive in your own life, and you aren't doing that right now."

"I'm doing what I want. I'm working on my art to display and sell during the Fourth of July celebrations. I don't need to do anything else. I definitely don't need to go off somewhere for any drinking or drug therapy. I don't have a drinking or drug problem."

"Come on, Caleb, please consider it," Johnny said and held out the paperwork to him.

Caleb got up from the sofa. He slapped at Johnny's hand, and the paperwork flew all over the room. "To hell with you all. I know you all think I'm a damned embarrassment to the family and there's nothing more you'd like to do than hide me away in Kentucky. But I'm not going there. I'm not going anywhere. There's nothing wrong with me and no reason for me to go to Kentucky or anywhere else."

Before anyone could say another word, Caleb stormed out of the room and slammed the door on the way out of the house. "Well, that went well," Luke said dryly.

"I never should have agreed to this," Margaret said half-tearfully. "He's always been the most sensitive of all of you. Now he won't trust me anymore."

Johnny looked at everyone and shook his head. "He's a grown man. We can't force him to go anywhere or do anything." He heaved a deep sigh. "I guess all we can hope for is he'll eventually get to a place where he realizes he needs some help."

Luke was bitterly disappointed this had failed, but he wasn't really surprised. Caleb might be the most sensitive of them all, but he was also extremely hardheaded, like the rest of the King kids. Still, he definitely worried about what Caleb might have gotten himself into.

One thing he felt right now was the need to see and talk to Carrie. It was funny, but whenever he was upset or angry, he needed his friend, and thankfully she was always there for him. However, if he kept pressing the issue of finding and questioning Joker, he knew he ran the possibility of no longer having her full support.

At five o'clock he left his place to pick her up, with the plans to go to the café for dinner. Because she had to go to work in the morning, he didn't intend to keep her out too late.

It would be easy to grow lax with her safety right now. Nothing more had happened since the car wreck. But Luke didn't intend to become complacent. The man who had tried to kill Carrie was still out there somewhere, just like Big John's murderer.

Luke had taken it easy for the last couple of days, but starting tomorrow, no matter how much danger he might face, he intended to continue his search for the man who had killed his father.

HE WATCHED AS Luke King picked the bitch up and the two of them drove away. He'd been watching her comings and goings from the house for the past week. He wasn't interested in trying to take her down on her way to or from work. Most of the time she wasn't alone, but rather had her roommate with her.

During the past week, while the house was empty, he'd checked every door and every window, seeking a way inside. Unfortunately, there were good, sturdy locks on both the front and the back doors. Even most of the windows held good locks. He didn't want to break a window to get in—he feared any broken glass would tip her off and she'd run out and escape before he could get her.

He'd been positively gleeful when he'd found a window in the back of the house with a faulty lock. Yesterday while they'd been gone, he'd rattled the window in the old frame until it had jiggled unlocked. It led into the kitchen over the sink.

It would be relatively easy to climb into it and then jump from the sink to the floor.

He hadn't been prepared yesterday for her murder, but today he was definitely ready and eager.

He'd decided he didn't want to shoot her. Shooting her would kill her too fast, and besides, somebody might hear the gunshots. He'd much rather kill her up close and personal, so he had two deadly sharp knives in his pocket. He couldn't wait to sink them both deep into her flesh. His intention was to hide in a closet until she was completely vulnerable.

A giddy excitement roared through him. Finally, he would get what he needed—revenge for all the lies she had told him. He was aware that it wouldn't change things in his hard life. It wouldn't magically make things easier, but it would definitely give him the satisfaction he needed. She had to pay, and he was going to make her pay.

He'd wait until dark to make his move. Right now, he was hidden behind a bush in her backyard, waiting for nightfall. He was clad all in black, so once the night shadows fell, nobody would see him sneak across the yard and through that kitchen window.

He didn't know if the roommate was home or not. If she wasn't home, then it was her lucky day. If she was home, then she could become collateral damage. He had no reason to harm her, but he definitely would if she stood in his way of getting to Carrie.

He had already had to wait way too long for this. He wasn't willing to wait any longer. A sweet anticipation swept through him. Yes, tonight was his night to finally make her pay—and he couldn't wait.

Chapter Ten

Carrie didn't ask any questions of Luke until they were settled in a booth at the café and had placed their orders. She was eager to hear what had happened with Caleb.

On the drive to the café, they had kept things light. She talked about her late night at the hospital, and he told her about the new ranch hand Johnny had hired.

Now, Carrie's curiosity couldn't wait another minute. "So, how did things go with Caleb?" she asked.

A deep frown cut across his forehead. "It was a bust. Johnny found a good facility in Kentucky, but Caleb wanted nothing to do with any of it. All we managed to do was piss Caleb off."

"I'm sorry, Luke. I know how much you wanted to get him help," she replied.

"Ah, well. You know the old saying—you can lead a horse to water, but you can't make him drink." He drummed his fingers on the top of the table.

"Hopefully, Caleb will get to a place where he realizes he could use some help and reaches out for it," she replied.

"Hopefully."

They both fell silent as the waitress appeared with their orders. She had gotten a chicken salad platter with cottage cheese and chilled grapes, while he had ordered the heartier meal of meat loaf and mashed potatoes.

As they ate, she enjoyed him talking about the horse-breeding program that his brother had encouraged him to get together.

"I'm starting to wrap my head around the potential. Not only will it bring in a brand-new revenue stream, but I'm most excited for the kind of excellent horses I know we could produce."

"So, have you figured out how to get it all started?" she asked. She was thrilled that finally he was looking toward the future and not back into the past.

"I plan to start researching it all tomorrow," he replied.

"I'm so glad to hear that, Luke. I know it will make Johnny happy, and I'm sure it would have made your dad happy, too."

"Yeah, it would." His eyes looked clearer and more at peace than she'd seen them. "Mom told me Dad always enjoyed spending time with me in the stables. I've always loved being in the stables among the horses."

"Then maybe it's time you got back to the stables," Carrie replied with a smile.

He returned her smile with one of his own. "That's what I'm thinking."

"Tell me about horses… I don't know much about the different breeds and what kind you might be interested in. All I know is there are old nags like at the Dickerson ranch and there are good horses at your ranch."

For the remainder of the meal, Luke talked about horses. It was obvious he was very knowledgeable in the area, but what she loved more was the animation that illuminated his features as he talked about a subject he obviously loved.

He shared with her conversations he'd had with his dad about the various types of horses, their health and well-being. "At one time Dad called me his horse whisperer because I was spending so much time with the horses. The horses seemed to understand what I would say to them, and I understood them."

"All this time and I didn't know you had this hidden talent," Carrie teased. "What else have you been keeping from me?"

He grinned. "I guess you'll just have to stick

around if you want to learn the rest of my secret talents."

She laughed in return, but the truth of the matter was she wasn't sure how long she could stick around with him with their relationship remaining static.

She was in love with him, and if he didn't feel the same way about her, then she wasn't sure how long she'd be willing to continue to see him. It broke her heart to think about no longer spending time with him, but in the end, she'd have to make a decision that was in her own best interest.

They lingered over coffee and dessert, and when they got up to leave, she realized this was the first time they'd spent time together and their conversation hadn't been about his father's murder or who might be after her.

Instead, they'd talked about things people on a date would talk about. It had been refreshing not to discuss murder or attempted murder with their meal for a change. For just a little while, she hadn't thought about the fact that there was a man out there who wanted her dead.

The conversation continued to remain light and pleasant as he drove her back to her house. It was only when he turned off the truck engine and he was about to open his door when she stopped him.

All evening her love for him had trembled on her lips, had burned in her heart, and she'd waited for the perfect moment to tell him how she felt—and that moment was now.

"Luke, before I go in, I need to talk to you," she said.

He settled back in the driver's seat and looked at her. His handsome features were visible in the bright glow of her porch light. "Talk about what?" he asked curiously.

"Luke, I… I'm in love with you." The words blurted out of her and hung in the air for several long moments.

His eyes widened. "No, you aren't," he finally said, obviously appalled by her words. "Carrie, we've been spending a lot of time together and you're just…just confused about things."

"It's because we've spent so much time together that I know for sure I'm in love with you," she replied. "Trust me, I'm not confused."

"But…but that wasn't part of our deal. We're friends, Carrie. We're good friends, but it was never supposed to be anything more," he replied fervently. "Believe me, you're just confused."

"Stop saying that," she exclaimed in frustration. "You're right in that this wasn't part of our deal, but my heart doesn't care about our deal. My heart fell in love with you." Tears welled up inside her and burned at her eyes. "I love you, Luke King, and I think if you look deep in your heart, you love me, too."

"Carrie, I told you all along that I had no room for romance in my life. I made that clear to you time and time again. I need to solve my dad's murder before I even think about romance," he replied.

The tears spilled over and raced down her cheeks. She'd hoped…she'd thought…but each of his words broke her heart. It was obvious he didn't feel what she'd believed he felt about her.

"Ah, Carrie, don't cry. You know I can't stand to see you crying," he said.

His words only made the tears fall faster. "Don't tell me not to cry. Not only is my heart broken for me, but it's broken for you, too. Oh, Luke, if you cling to this idea that you need to solve Big John's murder, then eventually you'll push everyone who cares about you out of your life."

"It's something I have to do," he replied inflexibly.

"No, it's not," she countered with a touch of anger. "At dinner this evening, you talked about breeding horses, and it was the first time I've seen you really happy. For God's sake, Luke. You will always grieve for the loss of your father, but you need to move on with your life. You're stuck in revenge mode." She angrily swiped at her tears.

"I love you, Luke, and I was sure you felt the same way about me. If you don't love me, then I hope you'll open your heart to more than murder." She looked out the front window and then back at him. She had no more words to say. She'd told him what was in her heart, and now she just felt empty and broken inside. "And now I'm ready to go home," she finally said.

He nodded and got out of the truck. Moments later they walked silently up to her front door. When they reached it, she turned to face him once again. "Luke, I can't do this anymore," she said softly, wearily.

"Do what?" His voice held apprehension.

"I can't hang out with you anymore. I can't spend any more time with you, loving you, when you aren't ready to move on with your life, when you apparently don't love me. I just can't do it anymore."

Each word she said shot an enormous wealth of pain through her heart, but she knew in that same heart that she was making the right decision.

She couldn't keep seeing him day after day, spending time with him and laughing with him without falling more deeply in love with him. And he didn't love her back. She owed it to herself to get out now, no matter how painful it would be to no longer see him.

"Carrie, please don't say that." He reached for her hand, but she jerked hers away. Where once she had longed for his touch, she now found it too painful to bear.

"But…but I need you," he protested, his gaze appearing frantic.

"No, you don't, Luke. You really don't need anyone. You're perfectly satisfied with just you and your obsession. There's obviously no room for anything else in your life," she replied.

"But, Carrie…"

"Good night, Luke." She cut him off, turned back to her door and unlocked it. "I'm sure we'll see each other around town. Good luck with things."

Without giving him a chance to respond, she entered her house and quickly closed the door behind her. The tears she had so desperately tried to control now unleashed, pouring from her eyes as deep sobs racked her body.

Weakly, she leaned back against the door, crying at the death of her hopes and dreams where Luke was concerned. She'd been so sure that he loved her. She could have sworn she'd felt his love in his touches and seen it shining in the depths of his eyes when he gazed at her.

She couldn't believe she'd been so delusional. She'd been sure it was just a matter of time before he'd professed his love for her. But he didn't love her. He'd just needed her to keep alive his fantasy that Peter would eventually confess to his father's murder. He'd just needed a partner for his madness, and she'd been that for far too long.

With tears still streaming down her cheeks, she pulled herself off the door. She threw her purse on the sofa and then headed for the stairs. Sadness made her legs feel as if they weighed a hundred pounds as she climbed each step and headed for her bedroom.

She told herself she needed to stop crying. She'd always known that heartbreak might be in the cards with Luke. But as each day had gone by, she'd grown more confident that heartbreak wasn't going to happen. He was her person, and she'd really believed she was his person. But she'd been wrong…so wrong.

Dammit, she'd been so certain he loved her and just hadn't said the words to her yet. Her every instinct had told her he loved her. How could she have been so mistaken?

She reached her bedroom and continued to weep as she took off her clothes and changed into a nightshirt. Once she was changed, she sat on the edge of her bed and tried to pull herself together.

She drew in deep breaths and released them slowly. She finally stopped crying, but she wasn't ready to go to bed just yet.

Instead, she decided a talk with Emily might help. Emily would be sympathetic and a listening ear as Carrie talked about how she'd gotten things so wrong.

She knew Emily was at home and in her bedroom, because her car had been in the driveway and Carrie could hear Emily's television noise drifting out despite the closed bedroom door. She hesitated just outside and then knocked softly.

There was no answer. Carrie knocked again… harder this time. It wasn't so late that Emily would be sleeping. Still, there was no response from Emily. She twisted the knob and cracked open the door. "Em?"

Emily was usually a light sleeper. Carrie opened the door all the way and realized the bed was empty. Apparently, Emily wasn't home. Maybe Craig, Emily's boyfriend, had picked her up and she'd just forgotten to turn off her television before she left the house.

Carrie was about to leave the room when she saw the pair of legs protruding out from the opposite side of the bed. "Emily," she cried, her tears about Luke instantly gone as worry about her friend welled up inside her.

She raced around the side of the bed and found Emily unconscious on the floor. "Oh God, Em." Carrie fell to the floor next to her, her gaze immediately going over the length of Emily's body as she sought any obvious injuries.

She saw nothing obvious. Had Emily fallen out of bed and hit her head? Had she suffered some sort of a heart issue? At least she seemed to be breathing, although her breaths sounded weak and shallow.

Carrie needed to call for an ambulance. Frantically she looked around for Emily's cell phone, but it was nowhere in sight.

Realizing her own cell was in her purse on the sofa in the living room, she left the room and raced down the stairs. She flipped on lights as she went. She'd just reached the sofa when a noise from the kitchen drew her attention.

Three footsteps, and then he appeared in the threshold between the kitchen and the living room. She froze at the sight of him. He was clad all in black and wore a ski mask over his head. He held a wicked-looking knife in each hand.

"Hello, Carrie."

LUKE DROVE SEVERAL blocks away from Carrie's place and then pulled over to the curb in front of somebody else's house. He shut off his engine and then unfastened his seat belt. He couldn't drive anymore. A tight pressure filled his chest, and a range of emotions flew through his head.

He felt sick to his stomach, and a band of tension wrapped around his head, squeezing tightly. He couldn't believe how the night had ended. He couldn't believe that Carrie really intended to not be in his life anymore. How could she just cut him out of her life?

She loved him. Her words thundered in his head. He tried to tell himself she was mistaken, that they were just really close friends. But she'd been clear she wasn't confused or mistaken about her feelings for him.

He hadn't seen it coming. But now that he thought back on things, maybe he should have. Maybe he should have recognized that her touches were filled with love, that her heart was all in on him when she gazed at him. He'd obviously been obtuse in not recognizing what was happening emotionally with her.

After they had made love, he'd never had the talk he'd intended to have with her telling her that it had been a mistake. Now he wished he would have had that conversation with her the very next moment.

Dear God, what was he going to do without her? Who would he have long, deep conversations with? Who would make him laugh? She was the best friend he'd ever had, and he couldn't imagine his life without her.

He couldn't believe she had made the choice not to spend time with him anymore. His feeling of grief was profound. His heart was emptier than it had ever been.

What in God's name was happening to him? He'd stopped seeing women he'd dated before in the past, but nothing had prepared him for the kind of utter loss he felt at never being with Carrie again.

Whom would he think about first thing in the morning? Whom would he think about just before he fell asleep at night? Who was going to keep her safe from the madman who was after her?

His heart clenched with fear for her. If necessary, he'd be her bodyguard from afar. He knew her daily schedule, and he could follow her to and from her work. She'd never have to know that he was around, watching out for her.

Still, it didn't solve the problem with his heart. He was nowhere near ready to be without Carrie in his life. And it hurt so badly that she didn't want to be in his life anymore.

With a deep sigh, he started his truck once again and pulled the seat belt back around him. As he pulled away from the curb, his heartache rode with him.

Chapter Eleven

Carrie stared at the man as a million thoughts raced through her head all at the same time. Fear kept her momentarily frozen in place. Who was he? Oh God, what had he done to Emily? What was he doing here…in her house? This wasn't supposed to happen. She was all alone in a house with a man who wanted to kill her and a roommate who was unconscious.

Her gaze darted around, seeking something she could use as a weapon, but there was nothing. "Who are you and what do you want?" she asked.

Maybe she could get him talking and she could slowly get herself closer to the front door. It would only take her a second or two to unlock it and run. At least he wasn't advancing on her yet.

"I'll tell you who I am," he said. "I'm the man who is going to kill you."

"What did you do to my roommate?" She tried to keep the terror out of her voice, even though it screamed inside her.

"Ah, I was hoping the poor girl would be out of the house tonight, but she wasn't. Unfortunately, I had to give her a rather hard love tap on the back of her head to make sure she didn't interfere with my plans."

"So, who are you?" Carrie asked again, hoping and praying that Emily would be okay. His voice still sounded familiar, but she couldn't place it.

"I'm the man who you lied to over and over again." His voice raised a bit.

"Lied about what?" She took a small step to her left, moving closer to the front door.

"You told me she'd get better and she didn't. She didn't get better," he yelled.

"Who? Who are you talking about?" she cried frantically. "This has got to be some kind of a mistake."

"Trust me, it's no mistake. You told me after her stroke that she'd get better. You lied to me. Damn you for all your lies." He took a step toward her.

Terror roared through her, sending an arctic ice through her veins. She didn't know who he was or what he was talking about. All she knew was his knives looked deadly sharp and a sick rage emanated from him.

"I don't know who you are," she said and took another step, moving her closer to the door.

He shoved one of the knives in his pocket and then yanked off his ski mask and tossed it to the floor. She gasped in stunned surprise. Jason Cart-well. His wife, Elizabeth, had suffered a debilitat-ing stroke about a year ago, but with therapy the prognosis for her to improve had been good.

"Now do you remember me? Or do you lie to so many people you don't remember one of us from another?" he screamed, his face turning red with his rage.

"Jason, I told you Elizabeth should improve with therapy, and that wasn't a lie. Did you get her into therapy?"

"It's none of your business what I did or didn't do, but it is your business that you lied to me. She's like a damned baby. I got to feed her and change her diapers." He took another step toward her. "And you know what the price is for all your lies to me? It's your death." He lunged toward her, and with a scream Carrie ran for the front door.

Too late. She was too late. She didn't have enough time to unlock the door. He slammed into her back, grabbed one of her arms and violently flung her away from the door. She half stumbled over the coffee table. She fell to her knees and quickly got back to her feet as tears of fear half blurred her vision.

"You're going to die the death of a thousand cuts," he said, suddenly gleeful as he charged at her once again. He lunged forward, sliced her fore-arm and then laughed uproariously.

Pain seared through her, and she grabbed her arm, where blood had begun to flow. She released her arm and instead grabbed a throw pillow from the sofa.

He stabbed at her, and she used the pillow as a shield. As the knife buried itself in the pillow, he laughed again. "Okay, let's play," he said.

He thrust the knife forward, and once again she blocked it with the pillow. Stuffing began to fall around her feet. It would only take another stab or two and the throw pillow would be utterly useless.

"Jason, please… I didn't lie to you," she said tearfully.

"Don't tell me. I got to feed Billie like a baby. I've got to change her diapers. She can't talk…she can't do anything for herself, and damn you, you told me she'd get better." He used the other knife and lunged out to stab her in the lower leg.

New, excruciating pain shuddered through her, momentarily stealing her breath away. "You don't want to do this, Jason. You'll wind up in prison, and then who is going to take care of Billie?" she gasped amid tears.

"I'm not going to no prison," he scoffed. "Nobody knows I'm here, Carrie. Nobody knows I'm the one who wants you dead." His dark eyes shone with malice. "Carrie, Carrie, you're going to be deady." He threw back his head and laughed. He dived toward her and sliced her arm once again.

"Death by a thousand cuts, Carrie. I'm going to slice you up good before I bury my knife in your black, lying heart." He laughed once again. It was the sound of a devil at work.

She was now too far away to get out the front door. Her head felt fuzzy from the pain that burned in her arm and leg. All she knew was that somehow, someway, she desperately needed to get away from him.

The stairs. If she could just make it up to her bedroom, that door had a lock. She could lock the door and then scream out the window for help. She could barricade the door so he couldn't get in to hurt her.

Knowing it might be her only hope, she raced for the stairs. She got up five of them before he stabbed her in the back of her leg. She screamed as the excruciating new pain shuddered through her. She quickly sat on one of the stairs, whirled around and raised her legs. With all the might she had within her, she kicked him in the chest.

He stumbled backward and fell to the floor beneath them. "I'll kill you for that, you bitch," he screamed.

She screamed as loud as she could as she scrabbled up three more stairs. She had to get to her bedroom. It was the only way she'd have a chance to survive. She was not going to let this monster of a man be the death of her.

Her chest tightened. Sobbing pants released from her, making it difficult for her to draw a deep breath. *Somebody help me*, a voice screamed in the back of her head. But she knew nobody was coming to her rescue. Luke was long gone, and nobody else would be showing up.

The knife once again sliced across the back of her leg. *Death by a thousand cuts.* The words thundered in her head. She refused to let that happen to her without fighting back. Once again she whirled around to face him, only this time her kicks were directed at the knives he'd used to hurt her.

She screamed in both pain and triumph as her foot dislodged one of the knives. It flew out of his hand and clattered to the floor below. She was ready to kick at his other hand when a knock sounded at her front door.

Jason froze, and so did Carrie. And then she screamed as loud as she possibly could.

"Carrie?" Luke's voice drifted through the door.

"Luke," she screamed.

Jason leaped into action. He went back down the stairs and disappeared into the kitchen. Carrie's heart pounded a million beats a minute. She waited several long moments, still frozen in place and unsure if he was really gone or not.

Luke banged on the door frantically. "Carrie? What's happening in there?" He banged again.

Finally, she ran down the stairs, unlocked and opened the door, and then collapsed in Luke's arms as she cried uncontrollably.

"Carrie, what's wrong?" He held her tight. "Carrie…baby, you're bleeding," he said in alarm.

"It's Jason Cartwell. He…he was h-here. D-death by a thousand c-cuts," she managed to say between sobs.

"Carrie, where is he now?" Luke asked urgently.

She pointed toward the kitchen. "He…he went in there."

"Go sit down," Luke said softly as he drew his gun and then disappeared from sight.

Carrie took two steps toward the sofa and then fell to the floor, still sobbing from the pain that burned through her. She was crawling to the sofa to get her phone from her purse when Luke came back.

"Baby," he said and then scooped her up in his arms and placed her on the sofa. He pulled his cell phone from his pocket and called for help.

Once that was done, he knelt in front of her and checked out the wounds on her legs and arms. "Honey, do you have any bandages here?"

She nodded. "In my bathroom upstairs. But don't leave me here all alone," she said with a new panic. "He co-could come b-back." She grabbed his hands and held tight. "Please, don't leave me alone, Luke."

"Okay, I'm not going anywhere," he replied. "But you're bleeding badly, Carrie." His features twisted in anger. "Damn him for hurting you."

"He…he was going to kill me. If you hadn't knocked when you did, he would have succeeded." The words came out of her amid sobs. "Oh God, Emily is unconscious upstairs. He…he hit her over the head. She needs help."

A siren sounded in the distance, letting them know help was on the way. As they waited, Carrie told him more about the encounter with Jason.

The ambulance arrived first, before any law enforcement. Carrie insisted that they go upstairs and tend to Emily before they helped her.

They brought Emily downstairs on a stretcher and loaded her into the ambulance and then came back inside for Carrie. They got her on a gurney and wheeled her to the waiting vehicle. Luke walked out with them.

"I'll be at the hospital as soon as I can," Luke said to her. "I need to stay here and talk to Lane."

"Okay," she replied as the paramedics worked to bandage her wounds. He leaned down and kissed her on the forehead and then stepped back as she was loaded into the ambulance.

It wasn't until the ambulance took off, the siren once again wailing, that she wondered, why had Luke shown up at her place at all?

LANE PULLED UP to the curb just as the ambulance sped away. Luke was angrier than he'd ever been in his life. Seeing the knife wounds on her beautiful skin, hearing Carrie's cries of pain and terror, had stirred up a rage he had never known before.

"It's Jason Cartwell," he said to Lane the minute the lawman got out of his car. "He tried to kill Carrie. He attacked her with a knife and escaped out her kitchen window. He allowed her to see his face because he intended to kill her. We've got to go after him, Lane. Maybe he's home now packing to get out of town."

"I'll head out to the Cartwell place," Lane said. "You sit tight here or go on to the hospital and I'll contact you when I have him in custody."

"I'm not sitting tight anywhere. I'm going to get Cartwell. You'd better hope you get to him before I do, because I'm going to beat the man half to death for what he did to Carrie," Luke replied.

He didn't wait for a reply but instead headed toward his truck. Lane hurried to his car and managed to take off before Luke.

Luke knew the Cartwell place. It was on the outskirts of town, a ramshackle house on enough land for Jason to keep a small herd of cattle. Luke knew he had a wife, but he couldn't remember the last time he'd seen either of them in town.

As he drove, he wrapped his hands tightly around

the steering wheel. Carrie had told him why Jason had wanted to kill her. It had all been about revenge for her supposedly lying to him. It didn't matter what his reasons were—all that mattered was the man had hurt her. He'd taken a knife and had slashed into her flesh.

He had no idea how many cuts Carrie had suffered at the man's hand. One was too many. Dammit. Why hadn't Luke thought of getting her a home security system? He'd just assumed she'd be safe in her home with Emily there.

He hoped Emily was okay. Carrie would never, ever forgive herself if Emily wasn't. She would blame herself for whatever happened, even though it was nobody's fault except Jason Cartwell's.

Once again anger seethed inside him. He'd meant what he'd said to Lane. He wanted to punch Jason's face in. The thought of somebody finding her dead in the house shot icy chills through him. Thank God he'd returned to Carrie's house when he had.

He stepped on the gas, hoping and praying they would find Jason home, hoping and praying that the man was arrested and charged. As long as the man was on the loose, Carrie wouldn't be safe.

He followed behind Lane's car as close as he could. They turned off the main drag and onto a gravel road. The gravel pinged on the underside of the truck as he raced to catch the man who had tried to kill Carrie.

As they got closer to the Cartwells' property, Luke's heart beat a thousand beats a minute. They had to catch him. Carrie deserved to live her life without fear, and that could only happen if Jason was behind bars.

He breathed a sigh of relief as the Cartwells' house came into view with Jason's old, beat-up truck in the driveway. Hopefully that meant the man was here.

Lane pulled to a halt, and Luke parked right behind him. Both men jumped out of their vehicles. "I'll go around back," Luke said.

Lane nodded, pulled his gun and headed for the front door. Luke also drew his weapon as he rounded the house and found a back door. He stood next to it, ready if Jason should try to escape out the back.

"Jason, it's Lane. Come to the front door," Luke heard Lane as he yelled and pounded on the front door.

There were several moments of silence. "Jason, come to the front door," Lane called. He banged on the front door once again.

Luke heard a scuffling noise just inside the back door. He shoved his gun back in its holster, afraid he would actually shoot the man. He tensed, ready to spring. The back door flew open, and Jason came out.

Luke immediately tackled the tall, thin man to the ground. Jason fought to get free. He attempted to punch Luke in the face, but the blow went wild. Luke grabbed him by the arm and yanked him to his feet.

"You bastard," Luke said and threw a punch that connected with Jason's lower jaw. Jason reeled back, but Luke held on to him. He was ready to hit him again when Lane came running around the side of the house.

"Luke, that's enough," Lane said firmly. He grabbed Jason's arm away from Luke and snapped cuffs on Jason's wrists. "I'm locking him in the car. There's somebody else in there who needs help."

As Lane disappeared back around the house with Jason in tow, Luke entered through the back door. Somebody else who needed help?

The door led into a filthy kitchen. Dirty dishes were not only stacked up in the sink but also lined the counters and the table. Flies buzzed in the rancid-smelling air, and rotting garbage overflowed from a trash can in the corner.

He couldn't believe somebody was actually living here. He stepped into the living room and gasped. Jason's wife, Elizabeth, sat in a wheelchair. She was achingly thin, and her arms were taped down so she couldn't move them. Another piece of tape was across her mouth.

"Elizabeth," he said and rushed to her. As he tore the tape from her mouth and then her arms, she gazed at him with grateful eyes. "We're going to get you out of here," he said as he worked to get her free. "We're going to get you help."

All he could think about was getting her out of the hellhole of a house. Dear God, what had Jason done to the poor woman? How often had he taped her down?

The living room was as filthy as the kitchen. Fast food containers covered the coffee table, and trash was almost everywhere in the room. His heart ached for poor Elizabeth, who had been forced to live this way. He was sure Lane had called for an ambulance already.

Lane came back in through the front door, his features twisted into a frown of disgust. "Let's get her out of here and into some fresh air," he said.

"My thoughts exactly," Luke said, and he pushed the wheelchair toward the front door, which Lane held open. Once outside, Elizabeth raised her face to the skies above, as if thanking God for her rescue.

"Billie," Jason yelled from the back of the patrol car. "Billie, don't worry, I'll be home in no time."

Luke saw every muscle in Elizabeth's body tense. "He's not going to be home anytime soon,"

Luke leaned down and whispered in her ear. "And you don't have to go back in that house or be with him ever again."

Several sirens screamed in the distance. Jason continued to yell out the window to his wife as Luke kept a steadying hand on her thin, trembling shoulder.

Two patrol cars squealed into the driveway, followed by an ambulance. Luke waited to see Elizabeth safely loaded inside, and then he ran for his truck, eager to see the woman he most wanted to see.

CARRIE LAY ON the hospital bed in the emergency room. Dr. Morris had just been in to clean and stitch up all her wounds, and he'd finished up by giving her a tetanus shot and something for her pain. He also told her he was keeping her in the hospital overnight.

She'd asked him about Emily's condition. He'd told her that Emily had been hit over the head hard enough to knock her out, but she was now awake and, aside from a concussion, she was going to be just fine.

The pain medicine instantly helped and put her in a drowsy state. She closed her eyes and tried not to think about what she'd just endured and all the stitches she'd had to get on her arms and legs.

If she dwelled on it, she would only start crying again.

Had the police caught Jason? Had Lane been able to arrest the man? Or was he still out there in hiding…waiting for another opportunity to kill her? She didn't want to think about that, either. Otherwise, she would be terrified all over again.

Luke. She'd think about Luke. If he hadn't shown up at her door when he had, she would have been killed. He'd saved her life. And he didn't love her.

Hot tears pressed at her eyes. Thinking about him only broke her heart all over again. She tried to empty her mind from any and all thoughts. She allowed the pain medicine to drift her away.

She must have fallen asleep, because she came awake suddenly, her heart racing until she realized she was still in the hospital and safe. Then she saw him. Luke stood just inside the curtain that kept her bed private.

He looked stressed as his beautiful blue eyes met her gaze. "Carrie," he said softly and walked to the side of her bed. "How are you doing?"

"Much better than I was doing an hour ago," she replied wryly.

"We got him, Carrie, and I managed to get in one good punch to his jaw before Lane stopped me. I swear, I wanted to beat him to death for what he did to you."

"I'm glad you didn't. I would have really been stressed out if you went to prison." She knew the grin she tried to cast his way probably looked goofy, but at this point she didn't care.

"Oh woman, what am I going to do with you? I guess the only thing I can do is marry you."

She stared at him. Was she having some sort of a delusional hearing issue? "Luke, I'm sorry. I'm on some pain medicine, and I must have misheard you."

"Then I'll say it in a different way. Carrie Carlson, will you make me the happiest man in the world and marry me?" he said. His eyes gleamed with warmth…with what definitely looked like love.

"Luke, I don't understand. One of the last things you told me was that you weren't in a place for any romance in your life, that you saw me as a good friend but nothing more." She searched his features.

"Oh, Carrie. I've been such a big fool." He reached out and took her hand in his. "After I left your house, I pulled over and really thought about my feelings for you. I love the sound of your laughter. I love the long talks we have about everything and nothing. I look forward to seeing you, and I dread the times when we have to say goodbye. I was only fooling myself with the friends-only thing. I love you, Carrie. More importantly, I'm in love with you, and I never, ever want to tell you goodbye again."

Each and every word he said seemed to magically take away the pain of the multitude of stitches she had just received. Each and every word he said eased the residual terror that had fluttered through her even though she was safe in the hospital.

"Luke, I need you to do me a favor," she said.

"Anything," he replied immediately.

"Will you tell me all that again tomorrow when I'm not on such strong pain meds?"

"Honey, I'll tell you again whenever you want to hear it. Now, will you do me a favor?" His gaze held the warmth—the love she'd always wanted from him.

"Of course," she replied.

"Will you answer my question?"

She frowned. "What question?" she asked. Darn the pain meds for making her more and more drowsy as each minute ticked by.

"Carrie Carlson, will you marry me?"

"Yes, yes, I will." Tears once again burned at her eyes, only this time they were happy tears. They lasted only a moment before a new worry filled her. "Oh, Luke. You might not want me anymore. I look like a rag doll that's been put together too many times. I've got stitches in both my legs and my arm."

"Carrie, I didn't fall in love with a pair of legs

or an arm. I fell in love with you, and no amount of stitches is going to change that." He leaned down and took her mouth in a kiss of infinite tenderness and one that tasted of abiding love.

"Now, the doctor told me not to stay too long, so I'll be back here tomorrow when you get out of here, and then you're coming to my place after that."

She smiled at him, still half-unsure if this was a dream or not. If it was a dream, it was the best one she'd ever had in her entire life. If it was reality, then she was the luckiest woman in the whole, entire world. Her eyes drifted closed. She felt his warm lips graze her forehead once again, and then he was gone.

SHE AWOKE THE next morning to sunshine drifting through her window and her wounds all hurting at the same time. She'd been moved the night before from the emergency room to a regular room. She hadn't been awake long when Shannon Franklin, one of the other nurses, came into the room.

"Hey, Carrie. I'm so sorry to see you in that bed," she said.

"That makes two of us," Carrie replied ruefully.

"I'm used to seeing you taking care of patients, not being one."

"Trust me, I'd much rather be wearing my scrubs instead of this ugly hospital gown," Carrie replied.

"Well, you know the drill. I need to get your vitals, and then the doctor has ordered some more pain relief for you," Shannon said.

"I'm not going to say no to that." Carrie raised the head of her bed and then remembered the conversation she'd had with Luke the night before. Was she really an engaged woman this morning? Had Luke really been with her last night and professed his love to her? A wave of happiness swept through her at the very thought. Or had it been just a wonderful dream?

Luke showed up in her room just after she'd eaten breakfast. "How are you feeling this morning?" he asked and swept her forehead with his lips.

"I'm hurting and a little bit confused. Luke, this may sound crazy, but am I an engaged woman or did I just have a wonderful dream last night?"

He smiled at her, the smile that always warmed her in a way no man's smile had ever done before. "Well, I can't talk to you about the wonderful dream you had last night, although I sure hope I was in it."

She returned his smile. "You were a main player in it." Her smile faded, and she looked at him more seriously. "Did you visit me last night? And did you really mean the things you said?"

"I meant every word. In fact, I'm late this morning because I made a stop on my way here." He took a ring box from his pocket, and her heart instantly quickened. "I wanted you to know just how serious I was about what I said last night to you." He opened the box to display a beautiful princess-cut diamond.

"Oh, Luke," she said breathlessly.

"I'll ask you one more time… Carrie Carlson, will you marry me?"

"Absolutely, positively yes," she replied as her heart expanded with the depth of her love for him.

He slid the ring on her finger. "Now it's official."

"Looks like I'm just in time for the celebration," Dr. Morris said as he stepped into the room.

"As soon as she's better, we're going to have a big party," Luke replied and smiled down at her once again.

"Well, you can start celebrating a little bit now, because I'm letting her go today," Dr. Morris said. "All I need to do is check on her stitches and rebandage them, and then she can go."

"And then you're coming home with me and we'll never have to tell each other goodbye again," Luke said, making her heart leap with the happiness and the knowledge that the man who was her best friend—the man she loved—loved her back.

AN HOUR LATER they were on their way to Luke's house. They'd left the hospital and filled a prescription for pain medication. When the doctor had changed her bandages, Luke had seen all the damage Jason had done.

How could a man do something like that to a woman? Her pain hurt Luke, and all he wanted to do was make her better. When he'd left her house the night before and pulled to the curb down the street, he had thought long and hard about his feelings for Carrie.

In the end, he'd realized that what he was feeling for her was love, the kind of true love that he'd been looking for. She was not just his best friend; she was absolutely everything he wanted for a life partner. All the time he was telling himself he didn't have time for romance, he'd been in a romance.

He'd driven back to her house, eager to tell her how much he loved her, and instead he had found her bloody and terrified. Even now, with her safe and in the passenger seat next to him, he wanted to wrap her in his arms and never let her go. He never wanted to see her hurting again.

The things she'd said to him still rang in his ears. She'd given him a picture of himself that he hadn't liked. He still wanted his father's murderer to be caught, but he wanted to have Carrie in his life more.

She'd been right...everyone had been right. It was time for him to leave the investigation to Lane. And it was time for him to let go of his need for revenge—justice—and get on with his life, a happy life.

"You're very quiet," she said, pulling him from his thoughts.

He flashed her a smile. "I was just thinking how much I'm looking forward to having a wonderful life with you."

"Luke, I want you to be happy, and I want you to be at peace," she replied.

"I saw what revenge looked like last night when Jason came after you. I don't want to be that man. I've found my peace with you."

She reached out and placed her hand on his forearm, a familiar gesture that warmed him. "I love you, Luke King," she said.

"That's all I really need," he replied as he pulled up and parked in front of his home...their home.

The afternoon flew by. Lane showed up to get an official statement from Carrie, and as Luke heard every single thing that had happened between Carrie and Jason, he was awed by Carrie's strength and her courage in facing off with the madman.

Lane also told them that Elizabeth had been taken to the hospital. She'd been suffering from malnourishment and had been badly dehydrated. Jason had never taken her for any therapy after her stroke, but she was now set up to go into a rehab where she could get all the help she needed.

After he left, Emily called Carrie to tell her that she was doing fine but she planned to move back home with her parents for a while. She would pay her half of the remaining lease and make arrangements to move her things out of their house as soon as possible.

She had been apologetic to Carrie, but apparently her encounter with Jason had scared her badly. Carrie had assured her it was fine.

It worked out perfectly for Luke, who wanted Carrie to move her things into his house as quickly as possible. He wanted their life together to start immediately. With Carrie's permission, he would pay off her rent and arrange for her things to be brought here to the ranch.

Finally, things had quieted down. He made them a quick dinner of soup and sandwiches, and then Carrie took a pain pill and fell asleep on the sofa.

He watched her sleep, grateful that he'd come to his senses where she was concerned. It comforted him that she would fall asleep in his arms tonight and that she'd be the first person he'd see when he opened his eyes in the morning.

He'd realized the night before that he had loved her for some time—he just hadn't recognized it. He'd been too filled with his anger to see the love.

He wasn't sure how long he watched her before he

finally got out of his chair. He wrote a short note for her in case she woke up, and then he left the house.

His feet took him on the familiar path down the lane and to the stables. He flipped on the overhead light to ward off the coming darkness of night and then sank down on a bale of hay near the center of the building.

The scents of the hay and the horses filled his head and instantly evoked memories of Big John. This time the memories came without the enormous stabbing pain and anger, but rather they fluttered through him on lighter notes of shared laughter and conversations.

For just a moment he smelled his father…the fragrance of sunshine and the fresh, crisp cologne he'd always worn. A deep grief swept over Luke, a grief he knew he would probably feel for the rest of his life. He would always mourn for his father. There would always be moments when he would feel the loss of Big John.

But how lucky he'd been to have had as much time as he'd had with a man who had been bigger than life, a man who had been a good father and husband. How lucky he'd been to have had a father he loved and who he knew loved him.

Still, it was time to let go and make time and energy for Carrie and the life they would be living together. Eventually they would have children and he would tell them stories about Big John.

"Luke?" Carrie appeared next to him.

He got up from the hay bale and turned to face her. "Honey, you shouldn't have walked all the way down here," he said to her.

"I thought you might need me," she replied somberly.

He smiled at her. "I need you every minute of the day and night, but I'm okay," he assured her. He pulled her into his arms. "We're going to have a great marriage, Carrie. We're going to laugh and love and build memories every day. Are you in?"

"I'm in," she replied with the bright smile he loved.

He took her mouth in a kiss that held all his love and desire for her. His father's murder still wasn't solved, and he didn't know what kind of trouble Caleb might be in. But when he held her in his arms, those things faded to background noise.

He could have chosen to stay stuck in his anger and obsession with finding his father's killer, but he'd chosen love instead. The woman he held in his arms had pulled him out of the darkness and into the light, and he knew it was a light that would shine on them for the rest of their lives.

* * * * *

*Don't miss the next suspenseful tale in
the Kings of Coyote Creek miniseries,*
Gunsmoke in the Grassland.
*And be sure to pick up other
exciting stories from Carla Cassidy:*

Closing in on the Cowboy
Deadly Days of Christmas
Stalker in the Shadows
Stalked in the Night
48 Hour Lockdown

Available from Harlequin Intrigue!

COMING NEXT MONTH FROM

⬦HARLEQUIN
INTRIGUE

#2091 MISSING WITNESS AT WHISKEY GULCH
The Outriders Series • by Elle James
Shattering loss taught former Delta Force operative Becker Jackson to play things safe. Still, he can't turn down Olivia Swann's desperate plea to find her abducted sister—nor resist their instant heat. But with two mob families targeting them, can they save an innocent witness—and their own lives—in time?

#2092 LOOKS THAT KILL
A Procedural Crime Story • by Amanda Stevens
Private investigator Natalie Bolt has secrets—and not just about the attempted murder she witnessed. But revealing her true identity to prosecutor Max Winter could cost her information she desperately needs. Max has no idea their investigation will lead to Natalie herself. Or that the criminals are still targeting the woman he's falling for...

#2093 LONE WOLF BOUNTY HUNTER
STEALTH: Shadow Team • by Danica Winters
Though he prefers working solo, bondsman Trent Lockwood teams up with STEALTH attorney Kendra Spade to hunt down a criminal determined to ruin both their families. The former cowboy and the take-charge New Yorker may share a common enemy, but the stakes are too high to let their attraction get in the way...

#2094 THE BIG ISLAND KILLER
Hawaii CI • by R. Barri Flowers
Detective Logan Ryder is running out of time to stop a serial killer from claiming a fourth woman on Hawaii's Big Island. Grief counselor Elena Kekona puts her life on the line to help when she discovers she resembles the victims. But Elena's secrets could result in a devastating endgame that both might not survive...

#2095 GUNSMOKE IN THE GRASSLAND
Kings of Coyote Creek • by Carla Cassidy
Deputy Jacob Black has his first assignment: solve the murder of Big John King. Ashley King is surprised to learn her childhood crush is working to find her father's killer. But when Ashley narrowly fends off a brutal attack, Jacob's new mission is to keep her safe—and find the killer at any cost.

#2096 COLD CASE SUSPECT
by Kayla Perrin
After fleeing Sheridan Falls to escape her past, Shayla Phillips is back in town to join forces with Tavis Saunders—whose cousin was a victim of a past crime. The former cop won't rest until he solves the case. But can they uncover the truth before more lives are lost?

Don't miss the next book in

B.J. DANIELS

Buckhorn, Montana series

Order your copy today!

HQNBooks.com

Heartfelt or thrilling, passionate or uplifting—Harlequin is more than just happily-ever-after.

With twelve different series to choose from and new books available every month, you are sure to find stories that will move you, uplift you, inspire and delight you.

Get 4 FREE REWARDS!

We'll send you 2 FREE Books plus 2 FREE Mystery Gifts.

Both the **Harlequin Intrigue**® and **Harlequin**® **Romantic Suspense** series feature compelling novels filled with heart-racing action-packed romance that will keep you on the edge of your seat.

YES! Please send me 2 FREE novels from the Harlequin Intrigue or Harlequin Romantic Suspense series and my 2 FREE gifts (gifts are worth about $10 retail). After receiving them, if I don't wish to receive any more books, I can return the shipping statement marked "cancel." If I don't cancel, I will receive 6 brand-new Harlequin Intrigue Larger-Print books every month and be billed just $5.99 each in the U.S. or $6.49 each in Canada, a savings of at least 14% off the cover price or 4 brand-new Harlequin Romantic Suspense books every month and be billed just $4.99 each in the U.S. or $5.74 each in Canada, a savings of at least 13% off the cover price. It's quite a bargain! Shipping and handling is just 50¢ per book in the U.S. and $1.25 per book in Canada.* I understand that accepting the 2 free books and gifts places me under no obligation to buy anything. I can always return a shipment and cancel at any time. The free books and gifts are mine to keep no matter what I decide.

Choose one: ☐ **Harlequin Intrigue Larger-Print** (199/399 HDN GNXC) ☐ **Harlequin Romantic Suspense** (240/340 HDN GNMZ)

Name (please print)

Address   Apt. #

City   State/Province   Zip/Postal Code

Email: Please check this box ☐ if you would like to receive newsletters and promotional emails from Harlequin Enterprises ULC and its affiliates. You can unsubscribe anytime.

Mail to the **Harlequin Reader Service:**
IN U.S.A.: P.O. Box 1341, Buffalo, NY 14240-8531
IN CANADA: P.O. Box 603, Fort Erie, Ontario L2A 5X3

Want to try 2 free books from another series? Call 1-800-873-8635 or visit www.ReaderService.com.

"How did you end up on the Big Island?"

"To make a long story short, I was recruited by the Hawaii Police Department to fill an opening, after working with the California Department of Justice's Human Trafficking and Sexual Predator Apprehension Team. Guess I had become burned out at that point in investigating trafficking cases, often involving the sexual exploitation of women and children, and decided I needed to move in a different direction."

Elena took another sip of her drink. "Any regrets?"

Reading her mind, Logan supposed she wondered if going after human traffickers and sexual predators in favor of serial killers and other homicide-related offenders was much of a trade-off. He saw both as equally heinous in nature, but the incidence was much greater with the former than the latter. Rather than delve too deeply into those dynamics, instead he told her earnestly, while appreciating the view across the table, "From where I'm sitting at this moment, I'd have to say no regrets whatsoever."

She blushed and uttered, "You're smooth in skillfully dodging the question, I'll give you that."

He grinned, enjoying this easygoing communication between them. Where else could it lead? "On balance, having the opportunity to live and work in Hawaii, even if it's less than utopia, I'd gladly do it over again."

"I'm glad you made that choice, Logan," Elena said sincerely, meeting his eyes.

"So am I." In that moment, it seemed like an ideal time to kiss her—those soft lips that seemed ever inviting. Leaning his face toward her, Logan watched for a reaction that told him they weren't on the same wavelength. Seeing no indication otherwise, he went in for the kiss. It was everything he expected—sweet, sensual and intoxicating. Only when his cell phone chimed did he grudgingly pull away. He removed the phone from his pocket, glanced at the caller ID and told Elena, "I need to get this."

"Please do," she said understandingly.

Before he even put the phone to his ear, Logan sensed that he would not like what he heard. He listened anyway as Ivy spoke in a near frantic tone. Afterward, he hung up and looked gloomily at Elena, and said, "The body of a young woman has been found." He paused, almost hating to say this, considering the concerns he still had for the safety of the grief counselor and not wanting to unnerve her. But there was no denying the truth or sparing her what she needed to hear. "It appears that the Big Island Killer has struck again."

Love Harlequin romance?

DISCOVER.

Be the first to find out about promotions, news and exclusive content!

Facebook.com/HarlequinBooks

Twitter.com/HarlequinBooks

Instagram.com/HarlequinBooks

Pinterest.com/HarlequinBooks

YouTube.com/HarlequinBooks

ReaderService.com

EXPLORE.

Sign up for the Harlequin e-newsletter and download a free book from any series at **TryHarlequin.com**

CONNECT.

Join our Harlequin community to share your thoughts and connect with other romance readers!
Facebook.com/groups/HarlequinConnection